BABY ME
A DRAGONS LOVE CURVES NOVELLA

AIDY AWARD

Copyright © 2018 by Aidy Award.

All rights reserved. No part of this publication may be reproduced, distributed or transmitted in any form or by any means, including photocopying, recording, or other electronic or mechanical methods, without the prior written permission of the publisher, except in the case of brief quotations embodied in critical reviews and certain other noncommercial uses permitted by copyright law. For permission requests, write to the publisher, addressed "Attention: Permissions Coordinator," at the address below.

Coffee Break Publishing

www.coffeebeakpublishing.com

Publisher's Note: This is a work of fiction. Names, characters, places, and incidents are a product of the author's imagination. Locales and public names are sometimes used for atmospheric purposes. Any resemblance to actual people, living or dead, or to businesses, companies, events, institutions, or locales is completely coincidental.

Cover by Melody Simmons

Baby Me/ Aidy Award. -- 1st ed.

ASIN - B07MKVRSL5

ISBN - 978-1-950228-51-5

DARK FORCES DON'T WANT THESE
DRAGON BABIES TO BE BORN...

It shouldn't be a surprise to Azy that her pregnancy is... different. Everything else about her has been too. A girl from Chicago who is half mermaid and mated to a dragon Wyvern? Yeah. That's not exactly the kind of life she can talk to anyone about.

But she's only a few months along and already the size of a house, a really big dragon sized house.

She'll happily let her little ones take over her entire body if it will keep them safe from the woes of the world, which not only include the dark forces of hell, but also uninvited mermaids, a whole crew of wedding planning friends, and a bizarre prophecy.

Cage has been to hell and back for his mate, literally. She's finally safe and pregnant with his twins. He can hardly wait for his new little dragon warriors to be born.

But when evil shows up wanting to destroy his entire world he'll have to defeat his own fears before he can help his mate and children.

That means living up to his destiny to be the courageous leader meant to guide all Dragonkind in victory over their foes.

And becoming a daddy too.

A flying dragon and a mermaid can have children... or can they?

For all of us who are still pretty sure that we're actually mermaids~

When regular words fail,
try "rawr."
It means
"I love you"
in dragon.

~ someone hilarious

YOU LEARN SOMETHING NEW EVERYDAY

Cage and Gris stood back to back, or rather tail to tail, beating back a horde of demon dragons.

"We must be getting close to where they are keeping Portia and Zon. I haven't seen this many demon dragons together since we opened up hell itself." Cage blew a gust of wind under an attacking group and threw them into the air. Gris swished his tail neatly chopping off all of their heads.

"Yes, we're close this time. I can feel them." Gris's words were more than gut instinct, more even than a connection with his twin. Portia was close. Gris's soul shard was glowing like a streetlight.

Portia might not be Cage's favorite succubus, she had done everything she could to screw over his life a time or two, but she was the mate to two of his dragon warriors. They would save her.

If they got to kill the Succubus Queen in the process, then even better.

Two more gold dragon warriors landed beside them. A woman slid off each of their backs and all four joined the battle. One of the mates was a sun witch and she peppered the demon dragons with spikes of white-hot light, turning as many to dust as her dragon. The other was a mere human, but she was a serious bad ass with a pair of katanas.

They pushed deeper into the dark alley behind the now deserted souk on the outskirts of Dubai. Geshtianna had deserted her rooms in the six-star hotel after Cage had a little meeting with the sheik who owned it. Of course, by meeting he meant scare the shit out of the guy.

"We need to capture one of the talking bastard demon dragons to tell us where the hell they are keeping our kin." Cage called the instructions to the new dragons who'd joined the battle.

Gris snarled and destroyed two more demon dragons charging at them, defending a particularly dark corner of the alley. "Where the hell is your rogue black dragon friend? If we lose them again because of his cowardice, I'll hunt him down and kill him too."

Jett had been off the grid since the destruction of hell. However, Cage had gotten a text message from a burner phone that even his elite team hadn't been able to track. It had contained GPS coordinates for this alleyway and a note that had instructed him not to kill any of the demon dragons that could communicate. The sender had also said that those instructions were not the favor he was owed, but a warning.

The message hadn't said anything about torturing information out of a talker being off limits. Thus far they had only encountered and eviscerated dozens of really dumb demon dragons. Like really dumb. The only reason they were having success protecting whatever hid in this alley way was by sheer numbers.

There was enough of the enemy that Cage almost missed

his words. Gris had no choice but to shift. His Dragon would heal the wounds.

Gold light shimmered across Gris's body and he transformed. The blood that flowed slowed and new scales formed across the open wound. Gris growled and Cage breathed a sigh of relief.

The sun witch, mate to one of his warriors ran toward them and brought light to the alley way. Now they could all see the rest of the destruction. Including a human woman lying in a pool of blood. It was the badass katana wielding mate.

Oh no. Not a mate. Not when his dragons had only just begun finding the women who lit up their souls.

A deep wrench hit Cage in the gut. He could do nothing. Nothing to save this beautiful soul mate. What if it had been Azy fighting here at his side? He would never survive her death.

The witch ran to the woman's side and began performing CPR. She was joined immediate by the human woman's dragon mate. A young warrior not even yet in his prime. The dragon shifted into his human form and grasped his mate's hand.

Even as the witch worked hard to breathe life back into the woman the crystal at the injured woman's neck faded and flickered. There was so much blood.

"Come on, come on. Breathe dammit." The witch pushed on the woman's chest counting the compressions until the warrior grabbed her arm and gently push her away. All the color drained from his face as he stared down at his mate.

He leaned down and whispered in her ear. "Where you go, I go."

The last of the light in the soul shard blinked out and the

young dragon warrior fell beside his mate, still holding her hand in his.

Cage roared into the sky shaking the crumbling building. He'd lost two precious lives tonight.

The witch put her fingers on the woman's neck and then the warrior's. She shook her head and looked at the others in the group, sadness and shock on her face. "They're gone. Both of them."

A golden glow of light washed over the couple and swirls lifted from their bodies. The streamers of light sparkled and danced around each other floating together into the sky until their souls dissipated into the night.

Cage swallowed hard past a lump of guilt, fear, and sadness in his throat.

Dragons died in battle, it was part of being a warrior. Some were taken by old age, like his own father's death. But his father had been almost six-hundred years old and didn't ever have a mate. This warrior had been young, a hundred and twenty maybe a hundred and thirty years old. He and his mate had only been together a few months. His body had no visible injuries. Hers was riddled with her own blood.

She had died fighting alongside them all, and her mate had joined her in death.

Was this the way of the world now? A mate dies and her dragon does too? Did it work the other way around as well?

This changed everything.

The remaining dragon warrior comforted his mate and held her tight to him. He stared up at Cage looking for guidance, for a sense of what this meant. Cage didn't know.

"Take your mate to safety, warrior. Keep her close."

The witch peeked out from her dragon's grasp.

"You too, little mate. Keep your warrior safe." She nodded

and the dragon warrior grabbed her up in his great claws and took to the air, flying high, far from the danger and carnage here.

Gris groaned and rolled to his side, shifting back into human form. His wounds were mostly healed. "What happened? Where the fuck is that succubus?"

"She's gone. The sacrificial distraction. I doubt if we even discover the entrance to Geshtianna's hiding place, we would find her or any of the coven there."

Gris pounded his fist into the dirt leaving a crater. "She'll pay for this."

"She has a lot to pay for. Geshtianna will regret the day she allied herself with the Black Dragon."

When Gris saw the bodies of the couple, he visibly blanched. But he knew his job. He contacted another team of gold dragons in the area to come and meet them, to retrieve their fallen comrades.

"If Geshtianna or the Black Dragon finds this out, we all may be dead."

The team flew in quickly and headed off for the new gold Wyr stronghold in Spain. Cage wished he were on his way there, and back to Azy right now. He needed to hold her in his arms, rub her belly where their babies grew, and know that she was safe.

One of the dragon warriors stayed behind. "Sir. I have a message from Azynsa."

"Well, what is it?"

Azy had sent messages through his warriors half a dozen times when he had been in battle these past weeks. Her words of love would have been embarrassing if he hadn't been so tickled that she didn't seem to care that she made his warriors say adorable things like hope your kicking butt today or giving them a specific number of kisses, they were to give him. He could use her kisses and words of encouragement now.

"Yes sir. She said to tell you, and I quote, get your ass back home now."

That didn't sound good. Azy was the one who had postponed their wedding in the first place and sent him off to help Gris fight these battles. She said she wanted the Gold Wyr strong and whole before their Wyvern celebrated his marriage. If she was asking for him, there must be something wrong.

After the battle and the explosion, it wasn't likely there was a mirror or any other shiny surface around that he could either talk to her or use the First Dragon's sword to transport himself back to her.

"Gris, I need to fly. Azy needs me."

Gris nodded. "Go to your mate. I will continue to hunt Geshtianna."

Cage had no doubt about that. "I'll return as soon as I can with more dragon warriors." Unmated ones, he wouldn't take that risk again. "We will find your mate and your brother."

He and Gris clasped arms. "I know. Now, go. Be with your mate, Wyvern. I have a feeling those twin babies your having are going to be important to us all."

HE LIKES BIG BUTTS

*I*t didn't occur to Cage until he was somewhere over Egypt that he could have probably called Azy on his cell phone. He opted instead to ask the winds for an extra boost to get him home as soon as he could.

He got to Spain just after sunrise and followed the sweet and salty scent of his mate to find her in the secluded treehouse he'd had built for them instead of the palatial estate overlooking the ocean.

He landed quietly and shifted into his human form. For a moment he simply stood there, staring at her, thanking the First Dragon she was safe.

Azy slept, with her long black hair spread across the pillows, her dark skin glowing, her lush pregnant body covered in a light blanket. Wind and sky above, she was beautiful.

She was his.

He slipped out of his clothes and into bed with her, curling his body around hers. His hands wandered over every inch of her, softly, slowly. He should let her sleep, but he needed to feel her, assure himself she was okay.

Azy had been pregnant with his babies for approximately three months and he knew nothing about pregnancy, but loved how her body had filled out, her breasts had swelled. She had grown more lush in all the right places.

He'd been gone from her side for almost a month, hunting for the demons who'd attacked his Wyr, killed and kidnapped his people. In that short time her belly had gotten bigger with his babies inside.

Cage ran his palms over her body and swore he felt his little ones moving. Wasn't it too early for that? In fact, her stomach seemed about twice as big as it had before.

Azy stirred and rolled to her side. "If you rub my back, I'll love you forever."

He chuckled and started in on her shoulders. "You'll love me forever anyway."

"True, but if you get that spot in my lower back that's been killing me, I'll show you exactly how much I love you."

His fingers found all of the hard knots in her muscles and her groans of pleasure had him growing harder with each one. Rubbing her back wasn't the only way to relax her.

"Spread your legs for me, Azynsa. Let me eat that pretty pussy of yours. Then I'll fuck you nice and slow, making you come on my cock over and over. We've got a lot of time to make up for and I've been missing you fiercely."

Azy rolled in his arms and gave him a nice deep kiss. Although it wasn't nearly long enough. "You are a dirty dragon and I'd love nothing more than to let you do exactly that, but if I don't get up and pee, for the eleventh time since I went to bed, I'm going to float away."

Cage reluctantly let her go and Azy groaned as she scooted

to the side of the bed. She sat there for a moment before pushing herself up and crossing the small room.

His lover moved like she was exhausted. A sucking hollow formed in his chest at the thought of his mate suffering. Cage got up and waited outside the door of the little water closet and the second she stepped out he lifted her up into his arms.

She didn't even fight him, only curled her head into his shoulder and let him carry her all two meters back to their bed.

"Is this why you called me back, my love? Are you ill, is there something wrong with the babies?"

He hadn't noticed any aroma of disease on her, only the distinct scents of the two small lives growing inside of her.

The wall of leaves that surrounded the treehouse opened and a soft white glow pushed through. A beautiful woman in the flowing white robes of a nun and a dozen or so necklaces hanging around her neck that faintly glowed red, blue, gold, and green walked in and stood at the end of the bed. "Azynsa is fine. It's hard work growing dragon babies, and these two are in a hurry to get born."

A thousand conflicting thoughts shot through Cage's mind.

He and Azy were both naked.

Who was this woman?

Was she a threat?

Didn't he know her from somewhere?

He'd meant to growl the questions, but they stopped in his throat. The fear and anger rolling around inside calmed as if it were nothing more than a warm summer breeze.

Azy touched his cheek drawing his attention back to her. "Cage, meet Senora Boh. She's a midwife...for magical beings."

Huh. "I didn't even know that was a thing."

"Let's see how you're doing today, mamacita." She motioned for Azy to lie on the bed. Then a gentle wind lifted the sheets and pillows, arranging them so Azy was covered and somehow Cage's pants ended up in his hand, so he put them on.

"You're a wind witch?" He should have guessed that a magic midwife would have some powers over the elements herself.

She ignored him, which was fine since her focus was entirely on Azy and his babies. The witch measured Azy's belly by moving her hands from finger to thumb and counted. "No wonder you're exhausted, these babies are growing like weeds. Adorable little weeds. But it's tiring them out too."

She pressed her ear to a couple of spots and listened through the sheet. "Aw, there you are, little man. Now, move your bum off your mama's bladder. She needs her rest."

A visible bump moved under Azy's skin and she sighed in relief. If she hadn't, Cage would have been freaked the hell out by that sight.

"Good boy. You two take care of each other in there." That same soft white light emanated from the witch's hands and seeped under the sheet. "There. I've given them a touch of magic to help them sleep in a little while. It will give you two a chance to do some bonding."

Bonding sounded good. He'd do whatever the midwife-witch told them too if it would help his new family.

She stood and summoned a large cupped leaf on a vine over to Azy and filled it with a stream of water out of thin air. "Make sure you're staying well hydrated, mermaid. The water isn't just for you, your babies like it too."

As Azy drank the witch turned her attention to Cage. "They would also like to go flying."

"They would?" Talking to unborn babies must be a midwife thing.

"Yes, and anything you can do to make them happy, healthy, and strong will help." She waved him to the bed next to Azy and Cage sat as instructed.

"I'm not going to sugar this up for the two of you. It's been several hundred years since we've had a dragon son born, and decades since a dragon and a mermaid have mated. Your two little ones have taken up the challenge and are growing at more than twice the rate they should be. That's making for a difficult pregnancy, and it's only going to get tougher."

Azy took Cage's hand. He swallowed, shoving his own fears down. She was the one bearing the stress for the last month, worrying and growing the babies. The least he could do was pretend he wasn't scared shitless by the tone of the midwife's speech. "What can I do to make it easier for her?"

Senora Boh tipped her head and smiled at him. "Anything and everything to make your bond stronger. I suggest starting with a lot of sex."

Cage coughed and Azy had to pat him on the back. "Sex?"

The midwife had a definite twinkle of mirth in her eye. "Yep. Preferably in your elements. Good thing you moved your Wyr to the beach. Plenty of water, sun, and a lovely breeze here, don't you think?"

Cage lifted Azy's hand to his lips. It was no hardship on him to make love to his luscious mate, but he'd thought she wouldn't be in the mood. He'd been prepared to sacrifice and have blue balls for the next several months.

Azy had said she wanted him earlier but had also put him off. He slid one hand into her long curls, loving the touch of her, wanting to touch more. But only if she was up for it. He didn't want to hurt her. "Are you okay with this plan?"

Azy laughed and snuggled into him. "Dude. Why do you think I sent the message that you needed to come home ASAP? I had every intention of jumping your bones no matter what Senora Boh said after the appointment this morning."

Fuck, yeah.

"That is my cue to leave. But, Azynsa, you need to be connected to more than just your mate. I know you haven't always been able to make friends, but I want you to reach out to the other dragons' mates. Your happiness and well-being are the best thing you can do for your children."

"Uh. Okay, will do." The scent of untruth floated right out of Azy's mouth.

Cage should have warned her you can't lie to a dragon. Why would she not want to do as the witch instructed? He'd thought she was on friendly terms with... uh-oh. Cage couldn't think of anyone Azy was friends with here in Spain.

The witch clucked her tongue. "Good try. But I've already sent for reinforcements. They'll be here later today."

What a douchcanoe he was. He should have thought to invite her Mami Wata sisters, or at least asked Ciara and Jakob to stay a while after they'd postponed the wedding.

No wonder she'd called him back from the hunt for Geshtianna.

His little mermaid lover wouldn't be lonely anymore. He was here for her now.

Azy sat up straighter in the bed, any calm she'd been holding onto totally gone. "Wait. What? Who?"

The witch smiled and made her way to the break in the leaves she'd come in through. She split them open wider and stepped out, floating in the air. "I'll be back in a few days to check on you. Oh, there's one more thing that can help. It will protect both your life and the babies, even more than great sex."

Cage shook his head. The witch was really stuck on the whole sex thing. She began drifting away, like a weird flying nun. "Find the ring."

THE RING

First, Azy had been gifted Cage's soul shard necklace, then the White Witch had given her another one with the miniature replica of her mother's mirror, and now she needed a ring.

Eyeroll.

Dragons and their shiny object hoards.

She pulled on Cage's arm and pulled him into the bed with her. "What's this ring thing about?"

Senora Boh couldn't mean a wedding ring. Cage had entire treasure chest full of shiny golden rings. He could pick any one and give it to her.

No, the way she'd said "the ring" had a certain, well, ring to it.

Cage frowned and stood. He grabbed her hands and pulled her up too, letting the sheet slide to the floor. "Come on, my love. I'll tell you all about it later. First, I intend on following instructions to strengthen our bond."

He leaned in and nuzzled her neck, then ran his tongue over the mark of the gold dragon she had on her skin there.

No matter how many times he did that, it always sent her girly parts into party mode.

The midwife had said an increase in libido was a natural part of pregnancy. She didn't think she could want Cage any more than she already did, until he flew into the treehouse early this morning.

She was quite literally aching for him right now.

"I'll let you get away with avoiding that answer for now, mister. But only because you promised me some orgasms."

"And orgasms you shall have." Cage stepped out the same break in the leaves Senora Boh had and she heard the soft beat of his wings as he shifted into his gorgeous dragon form. *Come, my little mermaid, let's see who's wetter, you or the ocean.*

"You are a serious cornball." Which she loved about him. He didn't let that side of himself out that often. The destruction of his home in The Netherlands, the move to Spain, the hunt for the succubus queen, and rebuilding the Wyr all weighed heavy on him.

She would do everything she could not to let anything stress him out even more. Even if that meant pretending, she wasn't freaked out about becoming a mother or that the midwife had invited people to their home.

Azy simply wanted to bask in the warmth and love of her dragon now.

She went to the ledge of their secluded treehouse and climbed into his outstretched claw, holding on tight to his leg. He cupped her gently and flew in long arching circles toward the beach below. She still wasn't entirely over her fear of heights, but as long as she concentrated on being in Cage's care instead of how far down the ground seemed, she enjoyed flying with him.

A warmth spread across her belly. Joy, like a soft giggle

spread through her and she couldn't help but laugh out loud. "Senora Boh was right. The babies love this. Go a little higher."

Cage gripped her tighter and caught an updraft, soaring toward the sun. With every foot they gained in altitude the happiness of the babies pulsed through her until she felt she could fly herself.

I feel their little spirits as if they were flying here beside me. It's incredible. Cage's voice in her head was filled with awe.

They flew through the clouds and were joined by several other gold dragons who appeared to be both enjoying the flight and also surrounding them in a protective pattern. After about a half an hour, the excitement and wiggling of the babies inside of her settled down.

She rubbed a hand over the swell. "I think they've fallen asleep."

Hmm. His tone had gone dark and husky. *Then, it's time for mommy and daddy to have their fun.*

Cage took them down and glided low over the water. Azy reached her fingers out and skimmed them through the cool ocean waves, then dove in, shifting from legs to her gold and white scaled tail in a breath. She already knew the water calmed the babies and she spent hours in the ocean every day, especially when her emotions got the best of her and she missed having Cage by her side and in her bed.

Those days she'd swim to the little secluded cove they'd found one of their first weeks here. She headed there now, because for the first time in a month, she wouldn't have to be there alone.

Her dragon was floating on his back sunning himself, his wings dangled down into the water. Azy swirled around, tickling the fine skin with her tail. His rumbling laugh reverberated through the water.

Come up here and let me tickle you. With my tongue.

Azy popped her head up right next to his ear. "Dirty dragon."

They both shifted into their human bodies and swam the few yards toward the shore. The second they reached the large smooth rocks that formed submerged benches, Cage grabbed her up into his arms and licked and kissed his way from her neck to her breasts.

Azy pushed her fingers into his hair and reveled in the feeling of having his mouth on her again. "I've missed you so much."

He growled a response, sending vibrations from her nipple straight to her clit. Then he reached between her legs and stroked her, making her gasp at his perfect, sensual touch.

His hands knew all the right places to set her on fire, to make her need him even more than she already did. Her body was so hungry for him, so needy.

Cage sucked and pulled on her nipple, then switched to the other one, tugging and licking it. She was so sensitive she could probably come just from that. But then he slid two fingers inside of her and found her g-spot, driving her soaring toward orgasm.

"Ooh, yes, Cage. More. More." Not like she had to ask, he knew how to make her come. Which was exactly what he made her do when he flicked his thumb over her clit. Azy arched her back and let the orgasm wash over her in waves as strong as an ocean storm.

Cage licked his way back up her neck and whispered in her ear as she shook. "That's it, love. Ride my fingers. Fuck, you're beautiful when you come."

He didn't stop stroking her, drawing the orgasm out, until her body went limp and she curled into his shoulder, spent.

"Mmm. I think you needed that even more than I did. I'm sorry I was gone so long. I won't be again." Cage settled back against the rocks and placed her on his lap.

"If that's how you apologize, I just may send you away more often." She wasn't mad. He was a warrior and a leader. He had more than only her to take care of, she understood that. It had been the same with her father. When it was time to serve and protect, that's what men like the two of them did.

Didn't mean she wasn't lonely when he was gone.

Azy let the water soothe and re-energize her then reached between them and found Cage's hard cock. "Now, let me show you how much I missed having you around."

She slipped off his lap and under the water. Being a mermaid had its advantages. The water filled her lungs, just the same way the air did, and she took him into her mouth, using her tongue to tease and tantalize him.

Even through the water she could hear his low, deep groan. She licked and sucked on him until his legs were shaking. She loved that she could turn him into a quivering pile of lust and give him as much pleasure as he did her.

"Azy, come back up here and let me fuck you before I explode."

How could she say no to that?

He didn't wait for her response and dragged her body up his, wrapping her legs around his waist. They both had to maneuver a bit to accommodate her round belly. He leaned back so that she was straddling him cowgirl style.

She didn't even have to move. Cage pushed in, a long, slow, deep thrust, filling her, making her cry his name.

"Cage, God yes. Fuck me."

His cock filled her, pushing her body toward another orgasm. "Say it again, Azynsa. I love your dirty fucking mouth."

"Fuck me, lover. Make me yours."

He dug his fingers into her hips, as he thrust up and into her over and over. "Yes. You are mine. All mine. Mine."

She loved hearing that. She loved being his. Loved him.

That made this so much more than fucking. They might get kinky, they might be dirty, but they both knew they were making love.

"Your pussy is squeezing me so tight. I'm fucking close, but there is no way I'm coming until you do again."

"Make me, dirty dragon."

Ooh. That glint in his eye told she was in trouble now. The best kind of trouble.

Cage pulled out of her and flipped her around, so she was facing the rocks. "Put your hands on them and don't move unless I tell you to."

Cage was the only person who she'd ever let boss her around like that. She secretly loved when he took charge and got all dominant and alpha on her. He enjoyed their roles just as much when she wasn't completely submissive to him. Her dragon loved a challenge.

"Make me."

He rumbled low and pressed his body up to her back, grabbing her wrists and shoving her hands flat against the rocks, caging her in with his arms and chest. "Naughty mermaid. Now, show me that juicy ass of yours."

She wiggled her butt against his erection and in response he leaned in and bit her shoulder, right at the mark. That shot spikes of pleasure through her. He bit and suckled as he slid into her pussy from behind and began fucking her hard. She'd pushed him into claiming her again and she reveled in his possession of her, the recreation of that bond between them.

Soon she was gasping for breath and moaning uncontrollably. "Come on, Cage. Explode for me. Make me—"

He gave her on final nip on her neck and then lifted his head and whispered in her ear. "Oh, I'll make you come."

His hand slid over her ass and he pressed a finger into her tight ring of muscles, thrusting in and out in time to his cock in her pussy. She cried out and her body burst into an intense climax.

Cage roared and pushed into her pussy as far as he could go, spilling himself deep in her body. They stayed locked together floating in the bliss they'd brought each other until Cage picked her up and carried her to the shore. He settled them under a tree, wrapping his arms around her and nuzzling her hair.

"I didn't mean to be so rough, love. Are you okay?"

Uh. Duh. She was great, and she loved when he lost his control like that, lost himself in the moment. "It was perfect. I'm pregnant, but I'm still the tough girl from Chicago who knows how to punch a lionfish in the face. You won't break me, Cage."

He laughed. "Not a shark?"

"No, they're like big dumb meat-eating cows that happen to have sharp teeth. They've got a bad rep is all. But lionfish are stuck-up nasty little mother-fuckers who will sting you out of spite."

"Aww, that mouth." He kissed her until she was ready to get busy with him again.

But first, while she had him all relaxed and pliant, she wanted to know about that ring…and why he'd avoided the subject.

"You want some more fun, big guy, first you tell me about the ring."

Cage pursed his lips together making a face at her.

She knew how to make him talk. Droplets of water clung to her skin and she swirled her fingers through them, gathering the water and wet first one nipple, then the other. Cage's scowl turned to interest at the way she was playing with herself, and he reached for her.

"You tell me about the ring, and I'll do more than play with my nipples for you."

He chuckled and cupped her breasts in his hands over hers anyway. "The witch must mean the Wyvern mate's ring. But I don't understand how she would know about that. Only Wyverns and their mates have ever had access to those rituals."

She slipped her hands from his and pressed her fingers against his chest. "What rituals?"

"It's something from long ago, and all of us had forgotten about it except for Match. Until Ciara showed up."

Ciara had been the first mate of a dragon in almost six-hundred years. She was a really nice woman, if a little pushy about wanting to plan a wedding for Azy and Cage. She, nor Jada, the Blue Dragon Wyvern's mate had mentioned a ritual. "Go on."

Cage looked out at the ocean. "Just who is this Senora Boh? Where did you meet her?"

Wow. He really didn't want to talk about this. She'd let him continue to avoid for now because if there was something he didn't want to tell her, it had to be a big deal. They were open with each other and he'd eventually tell her once he figured out how. "She said you wouldn't remember her."

"I don't know that woman. What if she was sent by Geshtianna or the Black Witch?"

"Sweetheart. She's been nothing but kind and helpful. Besides, she said she was the midwife who helped your mother when you were born. She said she's been at all the Wyvern's births."

He shook his head and growled, his dragon surprisingly close to the surface. "How do you know? How can you trust her?"

A wave of heat washed across the both of them and they were no longer alone. *Because I was at your birth too, and there is only one midwife who attends to dragons.*

A huge red dragon jumped down from a wall of rocks and lumbered toward the water. He was covered in ash and burns.

"Match. Where the hell have you been, man?"

Match. The Red Dragon Wyvern who'd been missing since Azy had been in Hell. She'd seen him once, the day she'd gotten Cage's shard from the succubus.

He'd been dying. Poisoned by her friend Fallyn.

Cage stood and pushed Azy behind him. What, like he was going to be able to block her and her big ole belly from Match's view. Yeah, maybe if there were two of him.

Azy didn't know Match from any other red dragon, but she worried about the fragile minded woman she'd rescued or rather dragged out of hell. The puzzling, but badass guardian, Ninsy, had promised she would take care of Fallyn.

Azy couldn't remember why, but she trusted Ninsy.

Match made his way into the ocean and rolled in the wet sand, washing away the grime from what looked like a battle.

Azy asked the water to cool and soothe his burns and pulled tendrils up to rinse the soot from his face.

"Don't bother helping this grumpy bastard. He's not a big

fan of mates." Cage crossed his arms and continued to put himself between her and the red dragon.

Match growled, but not at her. In another minute he made his way back to the land and shifted as he walked out of the surf.

Dear God. He was striking. Dark hair and sexy-ass well-kept facial hair. What surprised her the most was his dark olive skin. He looked more like he belonged in Spain than either of them. How was a guy from Poland this tall, dark, and handsome?

She'd expected him to look more like Cage with his fair skin and golden hair. Next to Match, Cage was as pale as a sparkly vampire.

"Ahem." Cage cleared his throat. "You're staring, love of my life, mate of my soul."

Oops. "No, I wasn't. He just surprised me is all."

Match walked over to the two of them and Azy found herself actually scooting behind Cage this time. Match might be movie-star good-looking, but he also looked mad as hell and very, very tired.

His anger lifted for a moment and he stared right at her. "Thank you, Azynsa."

Why did she get the feeling he meant for more than the cool water?

Cage wasn't the least bit intimidated by Match's hulking dominance. "Huh. I didn't even think you knew those words, dickhead."

"Your mate has done more for me than she knows."

"I have?" His gaze was so damn intense. He reminded her of a king.

"Yes."

"Well, good. I'm glad then. Now, shoo." She waved her

hands to get him to move along. This was her and Cage's special spot, and she'd had enough of this particular Wyvern's energy.

Match's brow crinkled, and Cage stifled a snicker. "You heard the lady. There's a guest room at the new villa suited to a red dragon, fireplace and all. Make yourself at home. You look like you could use about three days of sleep. We'll be along in a bit. I want to hear more about where you've been and that midwife."

Match scowled at Cage but then lopsided-grinned at Azy. He turned and made his way up the beach, stretching and yawning.

Azy waited until she thought Match was out of earshot before she said anything. "Holy anchovy, is he always like that?"

"A ladies man, you mean?" Cage was teasing her of course.

She pulled him down for a soulful kiss anyway. "You're the only man for this lady, and don't you forget it."

"I won't." He kissed her back, sliding his tongue between her lips and dancing with her until she pretty much forgot what they were talking about.

"We'd better get up to the villa before Match scares off all the staff."

"He is kind of unnerving, in an I'm-the-king-of-the-world kind of way. Is it weird that he reminds me a little bit of the Black Dragon?" She didn't think Match had an ounce of evil in him, but that potent power he possessed was something she'd only felt from one other being in the world.

Cage smoothed a strand of her hair and stared at it between his fingers. "Match is the Alpha of alphas. He's the first son of the first son of the first son a dozen times removed. The Red Wyvern has been the leader of all Dragonkind for centuries. It's a heavy burden he carries, and it makes him a cranky son of a bitch."

That explained a lot. "Dude needs a mate."

Cage laughed out loud. "It would take a strong woman to match Match. But yeah. We've all been saying for years that he needs to get laid."

"I hope he's the only visitor we have for a while. I was looking forward to some more me and you time." Azy waggled her eyebrows at Cage. As if he needed a hint at what she wanted from him.

Only all of his love forever and ever.

"Cage. Azy. There you are. We've been looking everywhere for you." A melodic voice floated into their little secluded cove. It apparently wasn't very secret anymore. "Oh. Eek. You two are naked. Gah. Sorry."

"Hubba Hubba. You were right, Ciara. Dragons are hung."

"Wesley, shush. And turn around, give them a little privacy. Sorry Azy." Ciara called down from the same set of rocks Match had crossed a few minutes earlier. "We'll just meet you up at the villa, shall we? I've brought dress samples, and Jada's already making cakes for you to taste."

Oh no. Not again.

The midwife did say she'd called in reinforcements. She hadn't said those reinforcements were wedding planners.

UNIVITED FRIENDS

*A*zy liked Ciara. She really did. Jada too. Fleur seemed nice, and she smelled good. Which was a bonus in her current state.

Over stuffed with cake and ready to throw up.

They were all having so much fun planning the most elaborate wedding that Azy didn't have the heart to tell them she didn't want one.

She wanted to be with Cage forever, and she was down for getting married even. But this whole wedding of the century? Ugh.

She spun in a circle trying her best to pay attention to each of the women who'd come to help her.

Ciara pushed half a dozen dresses around on a portable wardrobe rack and pulled one off holding it out to her.

"What do you think of this dress? This color is creamy champagne that is going to look killer with your skin tone. Ooh, wait, are you going to wear your hair up or down? Because that will make a difference with what kind of neckline you pick."

Jada stabbed another teeny piece of cake with a fork and held it up to Azy's mouth.

"Did you like the chocolate with the raspberry, cherry, or pomegranate? Because if you didn't like any of them, I've got vanilla bean with pistachio, mango, or lavender."

Fleur had flowers literally growing out of the floor.

"The blooms native to this area would look stunning laced through a wooden wedding arch. Oh, but that might not be high end enough for the Gold Dragon Wyvern's nuptials. I'll call around to hothouses and see what kind of fancy greenhouse varieties they have."

Wesley approached her with a measuring tape. "Sugar, I've got to get your measurements so I can make sure we've got room for that precious baby bump come wedding day."

How about nope.

Azy backed away from Wes and his instrument of torture. She did not need anyone knowing exactly how big her ass had gotten in the past month. She already felt like her stomach was about the circumference of the moon and that she'd look like a big ole pufferfish in any wedding dress, white, champagne, or polka dotted for that matter.

"I think I need a nap." Azy sighed and rubbed her belly. At least the little ones hadn't been poking her in the ribs today.

"Of course you do. We'll let you go, just as soon as you pick Cage's ring. Can we see yours, so we can match it?"

Sigh. This scene was like déjà vu all over again. Ciara, Jada, and Fleur had met their dragons, by way of a necklace that the White Witch had given them. Azy had not.

Ciara, Jada, and Fleur had gotten their dragons' soul shards, connecting and bonding them together after they had fallen in love with their warriors.

Azy had not.

She clasped the gold shard she wore around her neck now and pulled comfort from its warmth. Cage had given his soul's talisman up to a horrible succubus who was later forced to give it to Azy.

She and Cage had still fallen in love, and he had gifted her with his soul after a long battle with Hell. The end result was the same, but they'd taken a different path to become mates.

She and Cage had done everything bass-ackwards to get to where they were now. Looked like this was going to be another one of those times.

Azy was forever having to embrace her differences. Book smart instead of street smart when no one else in her tough Chicago neighborhood even cared about school or reading. Loving to swim when all the other girls at school were worried about getting their hair wet. The only daughter of a single dad cop. Different.

A chubby black mermaid who'd grown up in Chicago instead of the ocean.

Way, way beyond different.

No Wyvern's mate ring.

One more way she'd have to endure being different.

"I don't have a ring. The midwife said we needed to find it to strengthen our bond and help protect the babies. I don't even know where to begin. The White Witch isn't making this one easy on me."

Not like she had for Ciara and Jada.

Gah. She was being bitchy and wanted to blame it on the baby hormones. Azy blinked a half dozen times. Dammit. She was not going to cry.

Crab balls. A tear escaped and then all of a sudden she couldn't stop the waterfalls. She turned her head but knew full well she wasn't hiding her stupid sobs from anyone.

Ciara dropped the dress into a pile on the floor and rushed over to her. She took Azy's hands in hers and the tiniest fluffy snowflakes drifted down around them. "Oh, Azy. It's okay. Everything will be okay. You'll find the ring."

The words were sincere, heartfelt, and even though it was snowing, a calming warmth washed over her and settled in her belly. Her tears even dried up as quick as they'd come.

The underlying stress and emotions were still there, but Ciara's magic wrapped them up in a soft cloud, calming her. Azy stared at the blue-eyed blonde, a woman who couldn't be any more opposite of her own brown eyes and brown skin, trying to figure out if Ciara's gifts were also what made her feel a kinship with the woman.

Senora Boh had hit an old sore nerve when she'd said Azy wasn't good at making friends. From Chicago to the bottom of the ocean, she'd only ever had acquaintances.

Ciara squeezed Azy's hands. "There's no hurry. You'll find the ring. Jada found hers the morning she married Ky."

Azy's gaze snapped over to Jada who had a big silly grin on her face. "You did?"

"I didn't even know the Wyvern's mate ring was a thing, until I found it. I wasn't looking for it." Jada held up her hand and a brilliant blue band sat on her finger, sparkling like the ocean on a sunny day. "But the legend goes that only the true mate of a Wyvern will be able to find and wear the ring. It's pretty damn obvious you're Cage's true mate. You'll find it."

"How did you get yours?" Azy asked Ciara. Being the first mate of a dragon warrior in like a million years and all the White Witch had probably just handed it to her.

"Match challenged me. He didn't think I was a true mate. I've forgiven him for that, because I didn't think so either at the time. It was hidden in Jakob's hoard. That place is a mess. But I walked right up to it. I don't even know how."

"Cage's hoard is hidden all over the world. He moved most of it after The Lindens burned. Should I go look through what's here?"

Ciara shook her head and grinned like she knew something Azy didn't. "I think if we throw you this wedding, the ring will appear."

"Can your magic do that?" Azy didn't know what kind of powers Ciara had exactly, but it was more than what she could do with her affinity for the water element.

"Not mine, the White Witch's. She's the one putting us together with our dragons. I get a little blip of a vision each time she gives another woman a necklace and there's been a lot of them lately. Especially golds."

Jada put a hand on Azy's shoulder. "That wouldn't be happening if the Gold Wyvern hadn't found his mate. Now, they need their first lady. That's you or I'll eat my own choux." She shrugged. "What? I'm not very good at pâte à choux. Cake, yes, but French fluffy pastry? No. It's like actually eating a leather shoe but filled with custard."

"We just want to help. If I promise not to make this wedding bigger than Meghan and Harry's are you in?" Ciara asked.

Azy wasn't sure that was even possible, but it was so nice of them to care so much. "Of course. I appreciate you guys coming. It's not like I have any family who is going to show up or anything."

Funny that she should say that because just then family did show up.

"Azynsa. We have missed you." Three Mami Wata in human form, butt-freaking naked and still dripping wet walked into the dining room. The one in front, Zambezi, held one hand up, giving her the finger.

Azy covered her laugh with a cough. She'd told the mermaids that flipping someone off was a war cry of her people. After the battle to destroy Hell with the mermaids, many had taken to using it as sign of unity and basically, girl power.

Of course, Wesley chose that exact moment to walk back into the room and turned right back around. "Whoa. That's a couple too many naked ladies for me."

"Ooh." One of the other Mami Wata followed Wes, "He looks like mate material to me."

Uh. The Mami Wata hadn't contacted her once since they'd all battled the demon dragons and made the African coast safe again. Azy hadn't exactly reached out to them either. "What are you all doing here?"

Zambezi smiled. "We heard you will have a ritual to celebrate finding a mate. We would also like to find mates now. There will be potential ones at your celebration. You can introduce us."

"Wait, who told you I was having a wedding? I didn't even know until an hour ago." Azy looked at Ciara, but she shook her head.

The remaining Mami Wata dripped their way over to the table and picked up cake samples. Zambezi ate one, her eyes went wide, and she ate two more. "It's all over the ocean. Some of the mermen are very angry that we no longer want to have sex with them whenever they want it."

"About fricking time." The patriarchal misogyny of the Mer society drove Azy nuts.

"Yes. It is time for fricking. That is why we are here. Fricking, with dragons, or other men. We would like to have mates, like you, Azynsa."

Wow. Most Mami Wata had barely tolerated Azy, since she was only half mermaid and hadn't been raised with them. For them to admit they wanted something she had was kind of a huge deal.

"I can't guarantee you'll find mates, but I'd be happy to introduce you to some guys. I think Jada will know of some in particular that you might like."

Jada's eyes narrowed, and she studied the mermaids. She felt just as protective of the blue dragons as Azy did of the golds. "We'll see if the White Witch decides to match make for you three."

If she was going to have a wedding, there would be plenty of dragon warriors of all colors there. While she had a particular fondness for the gold ones, most of her sisters of the sea would probably be more suited to Jada's blue dragon warriors whose element was also water.

Okay, this she could do. If Ciara could tone the planning down, and it was just them, a few dragon warriors and a few mermaids, that wouldn't get out of control.

If one more unexpected guest came through that door, she might just call the whole thing off and talk Cage into flying the two of them to Vegas.

Actually, she might do that anyway.

Wesley speed-walked his way back into the dining room, no mermaid in sight. "Between the horny mermaids and the sexy ass Dragon warriors around here my heart is getting one hell of a workout today."

"Yeah like your butt needs more toning." Ciara rolled her eyes.

"Thank you very much. But I'm not the one who's going to be wishing she had been in training for a marathon."

"I can only think of one reason, make that two reasons, why I would want to run anywhere. Toward a good glass of wine or away from zombies."

"I know of a better one that might, maybe, definitely get your power walk on." Wes wagged a finger at Ciara.

Ciara rolled her eyes. "Not likely."

Wesley knew something he wasn't sharing, and he was having a good laugh about it at Ciara's expense. Azy could tell they had been friends for a long time. She hadn't ever been that tight with anyone.

Except, Cage.

Wes folded his arms and cocked one eyebrow. "Your mother's here."

Ciara blinked, stood up, spun on one heel and ran toward the door.

"Ciara Elizabeth Mosley-Willingham, you stop right there, young lady. That is no way to behave in front of your friends. Now, please come back here and introduce me." A petite, but curvy woman with stylish white hair, a silk dress suit, and a French manicure stood in the doorway that led from the kitchen. She tapped one toe and looked expectantly at Ciara's back.

Azy had grown up with only her father around and couldn't even imagine what it would be like to want to avoid her own mother like this. She did have to admit Ciara's mom was intimidating.

What kind of mom would she be to her own babies?

Ciara clenched her fists and slowly turned back to face all of them. She took a deep breath and then held out her hand, indicating to each of them one at a time. "Jada, Fleur, Azy, this is my mother, Wilhelmina Willingham. Mother, these are my friends. We're here to help Azynsa plan her wedding. What are you doing here?"

That last part had been said through clenched teeth and a dark little storm cloud formed in the corner.

"It's lovely to meet you all, I'm sure. What my daughter has failed to tell you in her brief introduction is that I own the most successful wedding planning business in the world. While I'm sure Ciara would do a perfectly lovely job, she should be busy planning her own nuptials. So, I am here at the request of an old friend to make sure this union goes off without a hitch."

Azy, Jada, Fleur, and Wes all exchanged looks. Wes was the first one to call her out. "Ciara, you and Jakob aren't married yet?"

Ciara suddenly found a spot on the carpet fascinating. "We'll get around to it."

Wilhelmina clacked her way across the room. "Yes, that's right you will. Especially since you don't have to plan this wedding."

Azy might not know what kind of mother she was going to be, but she knew what kind she wouldn't be. "Mrs. Willingham. I appreciate your being here to help, but it is important to both Cage and I that Ciara is involved. She has insights I don't because of her position and her powers. I know the two of you together will make an excellent team."

Both women gave her shocked looks, for very different reasons. Now that she'd gotten started on her little speech, she knew a way to make everyone happy. Including her.

"In fact, I'm so confident, that I'd like the two of you to just take over and plan everything. No need to even consult us. You'll choose better... umm, everything than I would anyway."

Mrs. Willingham narrowed her eyes. "Flowers?"

Azy waved her hand. "Whatever Fleur thinks best."

"Dress?" Wilhelmina's voice went up an octave.

Azy nodded. "I hear Wesley is good with a sewing machine."

"Food? The cake?" Soon this woman's voice would be outside of sound spectrum that humans could hear.

Azy grabbed a piece of cake and popped it into her mouth. "Jada's the best."

"Vows?"

Ciara interrupted. "That part of the ritual is already set."

"Rings?"

Cage walked in, looked around like he was assessing a battle and swooped Azy up in his arms. Her knight in shining scales. "I'll take care of that. Thanks. If you'll excuse us, I think my mate is in need of a nap."

Jada yawned. "Ooh. Is it nap time? Where's that sexy beast of mine?"

Ky appeared right on cue in the doorway. "I think it's well past your naptime, *aroha*."

Jakob and his second in command, Steele were right behind him. Someone must have sounded the alarm.

Mrs. Willingham scowled at them all. "Don't you all think for one minute I don't know what's going on here. I recognize a dragon warrior's retreat when I see one."

"Whatever do you mean, mother. There's no such thing as dragons." Ciara had gone from defensive mode to a scrambling offense in a millisecond.

"Good try. I'm not as sheltered and naïve as you think I am, dear." She walked up to Ciara and patted her on the shoulder. "I know all about the dragon warriors, their battles with the demon dragons and probably more than you do about being married to one, because I used to be.

Ciara's jaw just about fell off her face. "Mother. What are you talking about?

"I had quite the love affair with a gold dragon when I was your age. Although, I insisted we marry before we, you know." She waved her hands instead of finishing her sentence. "Besides, who do you think asked me to come plan the wedding of the Gold Dragon Wyvern?"

DRAGONCON

Cage gathered his brother Wyverns together when Azy went off with the women. He needed information and help. After what he'd seen in Dubai, he was not entrusting his mate's or his children's safety to a woman he didn't know.

He prowled back and forth while the other Wyvern's stared at him. They were all shocked by the news of a dragon warrior dying when his mate had. None had any idea what to do about it besides assign a lot of extra guards and keep mates far away from battles.

"Ciara is not going to like that. She fancies using her powers to smite those little bastards." Jakob was the first among them to be mated and had fought many battles against the demon dragons already.

"No, nor Jada. She's a very creative warrior."

Match had kept silent. "We cannot afford to lose every warrior who has a mate. There is too much at stake to let the Black Dragon roam free."

"I will not put Azy and my children in danger. If Geshtianna is working with the Black Dragon, she could have already planted spies in our midsts. Like this Senora Boh. Who the hell is she?"

"She's the midwife." Match shrugged and seemed distracted. "When a dragon is ready to be born, she's there to help them come into the world."

Cage paced while his brother Wyverns watched, not nearly as concerned as they should be. "Why have I never heard of her?"

"Because no dragons have been born in the past couple hundred years or so," Match said.

Wait, could that be right? Surely, there had. But there weren't any dragonlings in the Gold Wyr. "Ky, Jakob, you have young ones in your Wyrs, don't you?"

They both shook their heads.

Well, what the hell? A new fear grabbed at Cage's gut and twisted inside.

This was the first time in six-hundred years that gold dragons were again able to find their true mates. Many dragons of his father's generation had taken companions and those women had born their sons. Cage himself was the offspring of such a union.

But that curse had been broken, first with Jakob, then Ky, and now Cage. They all had no doubt now that the three of them had found their mates. The White Witch and the First Dragon would ensure that even a grumpy bastard like Match would find a mate so that the red dragon Wyr would be able to as well.

There must be more to the curse on them all than they understood if none of the dragons of their generation had children.

Their fathers hadn't had mates, but they had children.

Maybe the curse was evolving, and they had mates now, but wouldn't have offspring. It would mean the end of Dragonkind.

If the Black Dragon and Ereshkigal were behind this, affecting the future of all Dragonkind was a more devious plan than any of them even suspected.

The scent of his own fear burned in his nostrils. No, that wasn't his pungent emotion. He sniffed at the wind. Azy in distress, hit Cage causing his dragon to burst forth without him even needing to call it up.

Azy.

He and all the Wyverns moved like a well-oiled machine up to the dining room of the new villa. The other dragon warriors didn't even need to ask what was going on. Unlike generations before, the four of them had formed a pact. When one brother was in need, they had each other's backs.

Halfway there Jakob put on a burst of speed. *Something is wrong. Ciara is freaking out.*

Shit. Cage had never seen her do that. Ciara was the one who calmed everyone else down. The women must be in imminent danger.

A second before bursting through the door, Match blocked the entry way. He sniffed the air and then chuckled. *You do need to go in there and get your mates out. But carefully and I suggest in human form. There is something much scarier than demon dragons.*

Cage pushed, but Match didn't let him through. *I need to get in there. What is it that has them?*

Match stepped to the side to let them through. *It's Jakob's mother-in-law.*

Jakob shifted back into his human form and shook his head. "Shit on a shasta daisy flower. Ciara's mother is a great source of discord in her life. If we're going to save my mate and yours, we need a plan."

The rest of the dragon warriors shifted too. Match folded his arms. "I suggest a strategic retreat. Live to fight another day."

Together the four of them entered the dining hall intending to abscond with their mates. The second Cage saw Azy he really did want to sweep her off her feet and take her away from here. Mostly for nap. There were new lines around her eyes, and she had one hand in the small of her back. She was being questioned by a petite but curvy older woman with a screechy voice.

"Food? The cake?" This lady's voice was getting close to only being heard by his dragon ears, it was so damn high.

Azy didn't seem fazed by it, but Cage saw beneath the surface. Her scent told him that she was frazzled, tired, and confused. She grabbed a piece of cake and popped it into her mouth. "Jada's the best."

Aha. They were discussing wedding plans.

"Vows?"

Ciara interrupted. "That part of the ritual is already set."

"Rings?"

Cage walked in, assessed the best route out and picked Azy up to take her away. "I'll take care of that. Thanks. If you'll excuse us, I think my mate is in need of a nap."

He hugged Azy close to him, cradling her body into his chest. He could give a damn about the wedding. He'd do whatever Azy wanted. But he would not let some ancient ritual come between him and his mate.

"Are you okay, love?"

"I think our lives just got more complicated. We really need to find that ring and get this whole thing over with." Azy gasped at that last part and covered her mouth. "I didn't mean, it's just...I want to be with you forever, Cage. The wedding part isn't important to me. Only you."

Cage didn't need a ring to know Azy was his true soul mate. They rest of the world were the ones who wanted that.

Cage kissed her forehead. "Don't fret yourself. I feel exactly the same and I have an idea. Trust me?"

"Always." Azy glanced at the others and back at him. "Any chance that idea involves eloping to Vegas?"

Maybe it should. If he wasn't worried about her health on the flight across the ocean and most of the American continent, he'd take to the air with her right now.

He couldn't risk her life or the lives of their unborn children.

The conversation had continued, and he tuned back in just in time to hear that Ciara's screechy mother had been a companion to a gold dragon.

Strange.

It wasn't like Cage didn't know all dragons were total horndogs. He certainly had been before Azy came into his life. But he couldn't imagine the dragon warrior who would choose to make this bossy woman either a lover or a companion.

He couldn't think of any gold dragon living in the US then either. They mostly all stuck to Europe.

Must not have lasted, because they weren't together long if Mrs. Willingham had remarried and had borne Ciara. A puzzle for another day.

"Let's get out of here and I'll tell you my plans." Cage felt the tension slip from Azy's body. The more of that he could do the better. He wanted to get her back to the relaxed state she'd been in before everyone else started showing up.

"Yes, please," she said and nodded.

Ciara held up a hand silencing her mother. "Azy, Cage wait. Are you sure you want us to just plan the wedding?"

The two of them gave their response in unison. "Yes."

Jada snorted. "Like she wasn't going to anyway."

She lowered her voice and cupped her hand over the side of her mouth so only Cage and Azy would hear. "I think planning all of our weddings keeps her mind of the lack of her own nuptials."

She wasn't quiet enough.

"Ciara, dear. Is that true? Why are you avoiding your own wedding?" Uh-oh. Monster-in-law was about to go ballistic.

Ciara threw her hands up in the air and looked over plaintively at Jakob. "Oh, mother."

Azy poked Cage in the chest. "Now's our chance to get away," she whispered. "Go, go, go."

Smart lady.

Cage backed away slowly and when they were out of the dining room shifted into his dragon, then cupped Azy in his talons. He flew straight up and out of one of the built-in skylights strategically placed all over the house specifically for that purpose.

Azy was yawning before they even got to the treehouse and Cage dropped her right into bed. She curled into the pillows. "You don't think I made Ciara and the others mad by saying I wanted them to take over the wedding plans, do you?"

Cage shifted and stripped, crawling in beside her. "Ciara's probably tickled pink. She'll go completely overboard and love every second of it, I'm sure."

"Okay, good." She lifted her dress over her head and then snuggled up to him. "I feel kind of, I don't know, awkward around them. No one has ever been so nice to me for no reason."

That statement made Cage sad for the little girl she'd been. While he felt like he'd known her his entire life, in reality they'd only been mated a few months, and a big chunk of that he'd been away. He wanted to know everything about her. The good times and the bad, the things that made her happy and the sad.

He wouldn't be leaving her side any more unless absolutely necessary to defend the Wyr. Not after what he'd seen happen with the death of one of his dragon's mates.

What if he was killed in battle? Would Azy die too?

He couldn't take that chance with her life. As soon as he could get the order out, he'd make sure no other golds with a mate took chances either.

Regardless of what Match said.

How had dragon warriors survived for millennia? Maybe it wasn't a curse that they hadn't been able to find the match for their souls these last few hundred years. Maybe it was a blessing.

Cage couldn't figure out how he could be a mate and a warrior, or how he could be a Wyvern, leader of all gold dragons, if he couldn't lead them in battle.

He would give it all up for her. That wasn't an option. Being a dragon warrior meant protecting the world from the plague of demon dragons. Dragonkind had always kept humanity safe, they couldn't suddenly stop now.

Cage wrapped his hands around her and gently caressed her stomach. If it was possible, the bump felt bigger than this morning. Azy snuffled softly and shifted to get comfortable. She'd be the only one, because she pushed her ass right against his cock which was hard in an instant.

He would have liked to make love to her again, assure that she was safe with him, lose himself in her body. For now, he'd settle for holding her close. He didn't like the stress and exhaustion her body was undergoing.

Next on his agenda was to find that midwife and figure out exactly who she was and what in the hell was going on with his mate and his unborn children.

He fell asleep thinking about how to do that and awoke with a start what felt like hours later. The sun had barely moved in the sky and Azy still snored softly. Cage's mind and body were rejuvenated from his power nap as if he'd slept a hundred years.

He wished all the answers had come to him in a dream, but they hadn't. One thing had popped out of his subconscious though. The ring.

Cage knew how to get Azy a ring that might not have come directly from the White Witch, but from the First Dragon and that was the next best thing.

DON'T LOOK A GIFT DRAGON IN THE MOUTH

Cage stood on top of the highest hill near their home he could find. He wanted direct access to the sun's light and heat. The grassy knoll was unhindered by trees or rocks and the only shadows were from his own body and the sword he held over his head.

The sword the First Dragon had given Cage was shiny and strong. The magic imbued into it made it more than a mere weapon for slicing and dicing the enemy, it could move anyone he pierced with it through space when used in conjunction with Azy's mirror.

He sure as hell hoped melting a piece from the hilt wouldn't destroy the gift. The sword had saved his ass a few times in the past few months. Losing the ability to use it would be worth the sacrifice.

If his little plan worked.

Cage concentrated on the decorative metal on the hilt, drawing the power of the sun down into a hot ray, searing the metal around a particularly brilliant inlaid yellow diamond.

Even with all of his might, he'd barely melted a scratch

into the metal. If it took weeks to make the ring, he would stand here all alone, day after day until he had Azy's ring.

A strong breeze whipped around behind him and a dragon flew overhead careful not to block Cage's light. A lot of gold dragons would be flying in to Spain now that the word was out that the wedding was back on.

He could tell this one was a gold because of the way it flew. One of his wings was askew, somehow broken, but still he flew like a champ using the wind like only one who had the power over that element could.

It was probably one of his warriors sent by Gris to give a report on the hunt for Geshtianna. A broken wing telegraphed bad news.

The thought of losing more dragon warriors and their mates broke his concentration and the sunbeam he was using fizzled and dissipated.

Damn.

The dragon landed behind him and a voice he recognized from somewhere else sounded in his head. *Need help with that, son?*

Cage spun around just in time to see the sparkles of magic fade as the dragon shifted into a man. An unkempt warrior with a prosthetic arm sauntered across the grass toward him.

The man looked awfully familiar. Where had he seen him before?

"That sword was forged in a fire hotter than any on Earth. You're going to need more than some sunshine to break that diamond off for your girl."

"It's not just the diamond. She needs a ring. If the White Witch won't give Azy one, I will. She is my true mate and I won't let an old tradition stand between us."

These secrets spilled out of Cage's mouth. He wasn't

supposed to talk of Wyvern business with anyone but the other leaders of the dragon Wyrs and their fathers and sons. There were some things only first sons of first sons were supposed to know.

The fact that there was a test for Wyvern's betrothed to prove her worthiness to be the mate of the Wyr leader was one of those close-held secrets.

The old warrior folded his arms and nodded. "Ahh. You're after the Wyvern mate's ring then."

"Yes, sir." Damn it. He could not control his mouth.

"You think you can make her one instead of waiting for Inanna to leave it for her to find?"

That was exactly his plan. He couldn't wait on anyone else to keep his mate safe, warm, happy, and healthy. She was his responsibility. "I have to."

The warrior tilted his head to the side and studied Cage for a moment. Cage felt like he was being weighed and measured. He must have passed the test because the man nodded. "We'd better get to work then and make your lady something worthy."

Cage hadn't realized how worried he was about being able to create the ring on his own until the dragon warrior offered his help. He could have asked the other Wyvern's for help, but they had all sacrificed for him time and again. It was as if he'd been flying against the wind and now, he didn't have to fight anymore. He had no doubt they could craft a ring worthy of being gifted from a goddess.

"You worry too much, my boy." The warrior outstretched his hand asking Cage to hand over the sword. "You need to get back out of your head and start living with your heart again. Your heart is what connects you to your people."

What was that supposed to mean? "I've had a lot on my mind."

"I know you have." He turned the sword over in his hands and studied the hilt. He tapped on a particular spot just below the yellow diamond and blew a white-hot stream of fire at it. The diamond didn't budge. "You were raised to be a man of action. Nobody said you had to bear the weight of the world on your own."

Shock at this dragon warrior's abilities struck Cage directly in the chest like a big ole bomb of surprise. Gold dragons had domain over sun and sky, not fire. He didn't even know what to think about the man standing here on the mountain helping him, much less come up with a question to ask about why the hell he could control two elements.

He chose to concentrate on that rather than being called out on being a worry wart of a dragon. He and he alone needed to shoulder his responsibilities. That's what a Wyvern did.

The warrior blew another hot stream of dragon fire at the sword and this time a small gilded piece directly under the diamond melted enough for the stone to slide out of its place. Cage thrust his hands forward to catch it and had to toss the jewel from hand to hand like a hot potato. "Ow, that is really fucking hot."

He blew on it, calling on a little cool breeze to help him reduce the temperature to a manageable level. When he could hold it without third degree burns, he held the diamond up in the sunlight. So many facets reflected the sun into a million sparkles in the sky. Each of them reminded him of the sheen of Azy's scales when they shimmered in the water. "It's like this jewel was created especially for her."

"Maybe it was."

Cage gripped the stone in his fist, turning it over and over in his hand." How could that possibly be? The sword was created by the First Dragon hundreds of years ago."

The other man laughed. "I know. It has fulfilled many prophecies since its creation. Sometimes I regret putting it into the hands of your brethren over the years."

There was so much more to this dragon warrior than Cage had guessed. "You're the one who gave it to me, aren't you?"

The warrior laughed and rolled his eyes. "Duh."

Holy sun in the sky. Cage swallowed. The First Dragon, here, on a mountain top, as alive as can be. Okay. Be cool. There had to be a reason Cage was being blessed by a visit from his creator.

Why didn't he remember meeting the First Dragon before? The memory of receiving the sword was all a bit fuzzy in his mind. Dragons weren't known for wielding magic. Perhaps he was working with a witch. "The White Witch is the midwife."

It was too coincidental to have two beings interfering in his life for them not be connected.

"Figured it out, did ya? You always were smarter than you looked."

"I have the feeling I won't remember any of this conversation." Cage continued to turn the jewel over and over in his hand, using it to anchor him in reality.

The First Dragon slapped Cage on the back jovially. "Nope. Not a word of it."

This was completely surreal." Then I can ask you anything I want."

The First Dragon turned back to the sword and twirled it in his hands, examining the hilt." Hit me with any quandary you've got."

Cage would start with an easy one and work his way up to the tough questions. "Why did you give me the sword?"

"You needed it and it needed you." The First Dragon blew another stream of fire over the hilt and the sword split in two. Then he blew on it again and again until he held four pieces.

Cage watched in awe as his creator shaped and formed the metal and jewels into four new swords. They were smaller and thinner than the original, but still beautiful and equally as sharp and deadly as it had been when it was one. Would they work as the one had before, with the mirror, or did the new pieces have new powers?

"And because you and your brother Wyverns are going to need these." The First dragon handed one of the swords with a citrine in the hilt to Cage then set the other three down on a rock. One of the new swords had a sparkling blue sapphire, one a deep green emerald, and the final one a brilliant red ruby.

"Thank you, sir." The swords would come in handy when fighting the demon dragons and Geshtianna's servants of the night, but so did claws and teeth and tails. Without matching mirrors for their mate... unless the White Witch was with Azy right now having the same conversation with her.

"My mistake when I made this sword was to give it to only one dragon. Its power is too unwieldy, and the consequences of being used by only one warrior are too great. You've barely tapped into its magic and it's already changed the course of your future and that of your offspring. Just like it did my own twins."

"You had twins?" There was nothing about that in the lore, not that Cage had ever heard. Of course the First Dragon had sons. They had become the first Wyverns of each dragon Wyr, each taking on a color and an element as given to them by the

White Witch. But only the first sons of the first sons became Wyverns. If there had been a twin, where did he fit into the grand scheme of things. Was his legacy lost to history?

"Yes, my boy. Just as you are about to. One sacrificed his life to save all of Dragonkind from Ereshkigal's machinations."

The sadness emanated from the First Dragon and took Cage nearly to his knees. He'd never thought about the First Dragon being a parent. He'd raised an entire race of sons who were all warriors. Many had died in battle against the demon dragons. The thought of having to watch his own sons fight against the demon dragons and the King of Hell filled Cage with both pride and gut-wrenching fear.

Cage could hardly wait to teach his children how to wield their powers and destroy the Black Death, but could he handle seeing one of them die in battle? Fuck.

Cage remembered that the First Dragon had allowed him to ask whatever he wanted. "Sir, can you see the future, do you know what's coming? Will Azy and I lose one of our twins as you did?"

"Even Inanna cannot see that, my boy. We have been working at every turn to help you all prepare for the hard battles ahead. Kur-Jara grows stronger and soon even Ereshkigal's spells will not be able to contain the despair that has turned to hatred in his heart. You and your brothers have done a good job quelling the tide, but none of you can do it on your own."

"That's why the White Witch has been finding us mates, isn't it?"

"It's taken a long time for her to figure out ways around Ereshkigal's latest revenge."

A shimmer of light flashed beside the dragon warrior and

the most beautiful woman Cage had ever seen, aside from his Azy, appeared beside the man. She took his arm and snuggled up to him. "I couldn't have done it without you, honeybun. We make a good team. Now if only I can get your sons to do the same."

Uh. Was she talking about Cage? He and Azy were a team. They'd razed hell together. Literally. "We have done as you asked and worked to strengthen our bond."

They hadn't found the ring yet. Cage didn't like that the White Witch was denying that to Azy. "She is my true mate, my lady. You can give her the ring."

The Witch smiled and glanced down at Cage's hands. He'd fiddled with the jewel from the sword in his hand absently all this time. Sometime in his conversation with the First Dragon he'd forgotten he was even doing it. He opened his hand and instead of a faceted stone, he held a glowing ring that looked as though it was made of pure golden sunshine.

"She can find it in your hand just as well as any other place I might have left it for her."

Azy would love it and Cage could hardly wait to give it to her. "Thank you."

"Enough of the mushy stuff," the First Dragon said. He picked up the three swords and shoved them toward Cage. "Get a move on and get these to your brothers. You're going to need them."

That sounded a little to ominous. Cage shoved the ring into his pocket and took the weapons. A stiff wind whipped around him and he blinked at the bright sunshine on top of the bare mountain top.

Wait. Where had all these swords come from? They looked familiar. All four were similar in styling to the magical sword he carried. The one with the golden jewel called to him to be wielded. Suddenly he knew the other three were for each of the Wyverns and that he needed to get them to their rightful owners immediately if not sooner.

For the first time since he'd had his soul shard stolen, Cage wanted to go on the offensive against the demon dragons, the Black Witch, and that damned Black Dragon. He'd been reacting to the onslaught of dangers thrown at him.

No longer.

Now, with the four Wyverns gathered here in his new home, he had the perfect opportunity to man up and ask for the help to protect his family he needed.

For too long, he'd kept his fears to himself.

He shifted into his dragon and grasped the swords in his claw. They would help defeat many demon dragons.

Which was good, because just then, the demon horde showed up.

TAKE THAT, YOU WITCH

As soon as Cage got back from wherever the fuck he'd gone this morning, Azy was going to kill him. That was if she wasn't already dead herself. She crept forward into the darkened hallway of the villa. She'd barely made it in the door before demon dragons popped up out of the shadows. She couldn't go back, escape, they blocked the path behind her. She swallowed back the bitter fear in the back of her throat and inched away from the bastards. They weren't attacking, not yet anyway.

Everywhere she looked, the shadows darkened, and more demon dragons manifested. The normally warm villa felt too hot. Nothing moved in the air except the writhing of their scaly bodies and an occasional flap of wings. The silence surrounded her. So many things were very seriously wrong with this scenario.

Dammit. The villa and the area around it should have been safe and secure. Azy didn't have any weapons, not even her mirror.

. . .

THE WEDDING PLANNING-PALOOZA called her to come to the dining room where they'd set up shop. It looked like a damn wedding store in there. Even though she'd told them whatever they chose for decorations and food and even the ceremony would be fine, she couldn't begrudge Ciara her excitement. She was clearly having a blast going crazy with the plans.

Even Azy's Mami Wata sisters were thrilled with the whole idea of a human wedding. If the demons harmed any of them, Azy would march right back down to hell and destroy it all over again. With Cage's help, after the babies were born and hidden away from any and all evil.

Where was everyone? Had the demon dragons already killed, maimed, and destroyed them all? Where in the world were all the dragon warriors? They should be here slicing and dicing these piles of poo into underwear stains.

She wrapped her arms around her stomach and reached out to Cage with her mind, hoping against hope he was in dragon form. *Cage, where are you. Help.*

No response. Shit. No matter what, she had to keep her babies safe. That fear that burned the back of her throat bubbled up again. Azy had no idea how she was going to make it alone.

More of the stinking bastards popped up around her, hissing and clawing. Instinct kicked in and she punched the closest one right in the face. It retreated. Strange. Most of the rest of them backed off a few inches as well. That was the first one to even get close to her. She was open and vulnerable and surrounded. She should already be dead.

The masses of demon dragons scurried around her forming walls. No, not simply walls, a tunnel. They were herding her. That wasn't good at all. Fighting them all off alone wasn't exactly a choice. She certainly didn't want to go wherever they were trying to steer her. Who knew what would be waiting. Probably the Black Dragon, here to exact his revenge for the destruction of his hellish home.

Yeah. That had mostly been her idea. It had been the first time Cage had put one-hundred percent of his trust in her. She'd called together all their allies and executed the plan to destroy Hell and rescue her friend. There was no plan now and no one to rescue her. No allies. She was utterly alone.

Azy glared at the demon assholes around her and held up her fists to any that got too close. None made the mistake of approaching her again. With each step she took, they closed in around the way she'd come. The chill of fear for the lives of her loved ones seeped into her.

Please, Cage. Give me a sign. I'll make it through if I know you're okay. The warmth of Cage's soul burst against her skin. Its light protected her, pushing out warm rays that blinded and singed the demon dragons' eyes. They squealed and faced away but did not retreat.

She stroked shaking fingers over his soul shard she wore around her neck. At least she knew he wasn't dead. Cage may not be here by her side, but he was still protecting her. She wasn't alone, not with him as her mate. Okay. If she remembered that, she could make it through whatever was coming her way.

Azy called to Cage over and over in her head. Eventually he would have to hear her. As slow as the demon dragons allowed, she made her way through their deadly dark tunnel of bodies. They stank and hissed at her. Every time one of them made a move toward her, the babies would shift. They were smart little things and could feel the presence of evil around her. She did her best to soothe them with her thoughts and kept herself as calm as she could so they wouldn't be flooded with the tsunami of fear she was holding back.

In another few feet, the demon dragons skittered away and finally the bodies gave way to open space again. They'd directed her toward the great room where she and Cage had declared only the day before that Ciara and her mother could plan everything for the wedding to their heart's content. The two of them would be happy to simply show up. It had given them a reprieve from wedding planning hell. Now the room was a recreation of the depths of hell.

The room was dark and hot. The skylights were blocked and Azy could barely make out figures in the gloom and doom. Sweet seaweed in the sea. The Wyverns and their mates were all here. Ciara and Jakob were frozen in time near one doorway. Jada and Ky looked ready to pounce into battle. Match was literally mid-shift. His great dragon head already blowing a stream of fire suspended in the air, his body nothing more than a shimmer of red sparkles.

No mermaids, no other humans, and no Cage.

What the literal hell was going on here?

"Come in, young mermaid." At the long dining table, sat one witch Azy never thought she'd see again. Ereshkigal, the Black Witch, queen of the underworld.

"What do you want, witch?" Azy couldn't keep the disdain out of her voice even though she probably should. She was surrounded, powerless, with no hope of rescue.

The witch didn't seem bothered by Azy's animosity. She picked at some cake left on a plate near where she was sitting, poking at it with her long craggy-ass fingernails. Girl needed a manicure, bad. "There are many things I want, and I shall have them. You're going to help me."

Yeah. No. "Only if one of those wants is to die. I'll happily help you with that."

"I warned Kur-Jara that a half human mate's soul would be worthless to us. Especially one with no real love, no magic, nothing useful but a connection with the shard." The witch scoffed at Azy and waved her hand. She said some words in an ancient sounding tongue and the world around Azy went even darker.

The only light in the room came from the soul shard. The witch rose to her feet and glared at Azy. She pointed to the necklace and it floated up tugging at Azy's neck.

The witch's words burned into her. Worthless. No love. Nothing useful. A year ago, she might have believed those words. She had love. A love so deep and important it had completely changed her world. Cage's love had changed Azy, helped her find her own love for herself.

Azy reached for the shard, knowing that if the Black Witch somehow got her hands on that precious piece of Cage's soul there would be world ending consequences. The muscles in her entire body stung with the effort. She couldn't move. Her arms wouldn't respond. She could breathe, she could blink, but the rest of her body was frozen, caught in the witch's spell. That must be what had happened to everyone else in the room. This dark magic had stopped all of the dragons and their mates in their tracks.

All except Cage. He wasn't here. Thank Poseidon.

There was no way she could fight against magic this powerful. The teensy tiny bit of magic she had in her power with the water was paltry, and certainly not the least bit useful at the moment. Squirting Ereshkigal in the face with a bit of ocean water wasn't going to do much for their plight. Azy needed a miracle.

"Don't bother reaching for your power. None but mine will work here. The magic Inanna gave to you and your dragons can't help you now. Bah." Ereshkigal slowly crossed the room. "Don't worry. I don't need or want your souls anymore."

Don't worry? Ha. With every step the witch took dark despair dragged its ugliness across Azy's psyche. If Ereshkigal didn't want the soul shards what was she after?

"Inanna can have them. Just know she's never given anything that didn't have a price or that couldn't be used for her own gain."

Uhh. This vendetta the witch had went deeper than the battle between good and evil. Sounded more like a mean girls' issue or a family feud. So the drama. Azy did not want to be caught in the middle of a witch's cat fight.

Azy screamed inside of her mind as the Black Witch's hand extended and touched her belly. If she could move, she would first vomit all over the witch, and then kick her fucking ass.

"Yes, this will work out much better. Kur-Jara will never be anything more than Inanna's pawn, always wanting what he can't have. He's so like his father that way." Ereshkigal spit, like the thought of the Black Dragon's father sickened her. "No, if I want my revenge, I'll have to have a soul that hasn't been touched by her. Two souls is even better."

There was no way on this blue and green earth that Ereshkigal would ever be near her children. Rage built inside of Azy until her body was vibrating. A white-hot energy swirled from her belly. Wait. That wasn't her. The power was coming from her womb. A zip of electricity jumped out and snapped at Ereshkigal's hand and she yanked it away.

Holy electrophorus electricus. That had come from her babies.

That's right kiddos. You don't let anybody bully you. Azy had no idea if her children could feel or understand her thoughts, but she sent them mental hugs and kisses. She drew the strength they were emanating and together they broke the bonds of Ereshkigal's spell. In a wash of golden light, they were free.

"Ah, yes. These babes already have so much power. I will use up every bit of it to destroy Inanna and her precious dragons."

"Not on my watch, bitch face." Azy backed away, moving further from the other dragons and their mates. If she could draw Ereshkigal away, she could protect all of them. But then what was she going to do? She'd be stuck all by herself with the Black Witch. Bad idea.

She'd broken the spell freezing her in place, but that had used up a great deal of her strength. No way Azy was going to be able to physically fight. She narrowed her eyes and laid her strongest sneer on the crone while mentally cooing to her children and desperately trying to see a way out of this dilemma.

Come now, babies. Let's all call daddy together and see if we can't find his big ole dragon butt to come and help us out.

Azy barely placed Cage's name in her mind when his mental voice popped into her head. She could almost sag to the floor in relief.

Azynsa, love. Where are you? Are you safe?

Sort of, not really. We could sure as shit use some help. She sent him an image of the dining room and creepy Ereshkigal moving back in on her.

Do not let her touch you. I'll be there as fast as I can.

Right. No touching. That was the plan. Also murdering any demon dragon or witch who even thought about coming near her. For that she would need a weapon of some kind. Why, oh why didn't they have more swords, or guns, or hand grenades lying around the villa? Azy glanced toward the table and the only thing even coming close to a weapon was a cake server. She would hack a bitch's head off with that if she had too.

"Come now, mermaid. Your children's magic may have broken the spell holding you in place, but nothing can keep me from taking them back down to the underworld with me. Don't fight it and I will let you see them before you die." The witch snarled and lunged.

Azy shoved a chair between them, blocking the witch's path. "That's never going to happen, you whorebag."

"You can't stop it." The witch waved her hands and the demon dragons who'd all been lurking in the hallway poured into the room. They were followed by the tall creepy ass demons Azy had seen in hell. Annunaki demons, Ereshkigal's own personal judge, jury, and executioners.

Azy straightened up and put on her best bring-it-on face and tone of voice. Her secret weapon was about to arrive. "Wanna bet?"

Stones, mortar, wood, sunlight, and a really big, very angry dragon crashed down from the ceiling. Cage roared so loudly, Azy had to cover her ears. She'd never heard a more glorious sound. The Black Witch screeched in an I'm-melting, I'm-melting sort of way that was the second best song of the day.

Even while she screamed, the witch made the same movements with her hands as she had when she'd cast her freezing spell on Azy. No way, no how could she let Cage get caught by surprise like she'd been. Azy rubbed her belly hoping the babies had more protection for their daddy too. *Look out, she's casting a spell.*

A sharp wind whipped through the room picking up furniture and throwing it toward the witch. Ereshkigal cried out and raised her arms screaming for the Annunaki and the demon dragons. They swarmed into the room, a group of Annunaki putting themselves in front of her and blocking Cage's attacks. He roared again and whipped his tail at the roof, opening more holes and pulling the sunlight down in bright beams. He crunched a half dozen of the bastards between his great jaws and turned another group of them to black sludge with his claws. Still they swarmed in on him.

Ereshkigal slunk back from Cage's attack and narrowed her eyes on Azy. "Your babes are mine. Either I take them now or you can live in fear for the rest of your days."

Oh, hells to the no.

Little ones, daddy needs our help. I promise you a nice long flight with him and a soothing swim when this is all over. Even with the battle waging around her, Azy closed her eyes and centered herself, giving every bit of energy she had to her children. Sparks of white light shot from her body, zigging and zagging through the room. They didn't strike down the witch, or the demon dragons like she thought they would.

The light shot forward and into each of the other dragon warriors first, and then sparkled onto the rest of the mates and Wyverns in the room. Everyone came to life as the magic burst the Black Witch's spell over them all. Her smarty smart pants children had just turned the tide of this battle. It took the last bit of energy out of Azy. She wouldn't be able to fight or defend herself in this condition.

She hated to retreat, but it was time to let her dragon warrior take over the fight. Azy grabbed the silver cake server and scooted the nearest chair away from the big wooden dining room table to make room for her and her big belly. She hunkered down underneath of it, weapon held at the ready should any demon dragon deign to stick its nose in her direction.

Match was the first to come to life, instantly in his giant red dragon form. His flames incinerated a mass of demon dragons, turning them to nothing more than piles of inky black ash. Cage tossed some sort of a sword to him, and then more to Jakob and Ky. The four swords glowed with a light, matching the dragons' colors. Before everyone's eyes, the swords sunk into the scales at the tip of each warriors' tail, weaponizing an already deadly tool.

The warriors worked in concert, cornering and slashing their way through piles of demon dragons. Cage and Match were particularly brutal in their attacks. Any attempt by any of the demons to even come close to one of the mates, and Cage immediately eviscerated them. He was definitely gunning for MVP of the battle, quarterbacking the hell out of their offense. He was seemingly everyone at once, letting no harm come to her, Ciara, Fleur, or Jada whether by his own strikes or directing the other warriors. He was glorious.

But while Cage seemed focused and in control, Match was going absolutely berserk trying to get to the Black Witch. His fire filled the room over and over, taking out demon dragons, furniture, and wedding dresses left and right. A moment before he reached Ereshkigal, he shifted back into his human form. What the hell was he doing?

Match used the shiny new sword to lop off the head of the last Annunaki demon guarding Ereshkigal then lunged forward and grabbed the witch, thrusting her up against the wall. Smoke billowed from his mouth and nose. "Where is she, crone?"

He shook with rage. "You've destroyed her life long enough. She is mine. Where are you hiding her?"

Ereshkigal screeched with a sound louder than all the demon dragons combined and disappeared in a puff of oily black smoke that filled the room. Everyone coughed and sputtered trying to avoid breathing in the rank, thick air. Azy covered her nose and mouth, not wanting any of the tainted smoke reaching into her body and harming the little ones.

Azynsa, where are you? My wind cannot clear the air. Tell me you're okay. Cage bellowed into her head.

I'm okay. We're safe. I crawled under the table. Not a thing had disturbed her the entire battle and now it was practically over.

That's my smart mate.

A black scaled arm shoved her mother's magic mirror in front of her face. She jerked away, but the demon dragon caught her arm.

"No go. You talk." It shook the mirror at her.

Azy did her best to yank her arm away. She couldn't die now. That was total bullshit to survive this long and get dead at the last moment. "Fuck you. Get off of me."

"You talk. Jett comes," it hissed.

"Jett?" Did this asshole really think she was going to call up his friend for him?

"Jett comes. I help you. Babies live."

No. It couldn't be. This demon dragon was offering to help her and the dragon warriors.

DEALS WITH DEMONS AND OTHER THINGS THAT HURT

*A*zy snatched the mirror from the demon dragon and scooted away from him holding her cake server weapon out to defend herself. "Get away. You can't fool me. You aren't going to help us. What do you want?"

It snapped its jaws and snarled. "Jett comes. Black dragons rise."

That was the last thing Azy needed. "You can tell the Black Dragon to suck my dick."

The demon dragon slashed at a chair, cutting it in two with its claws. It crawled closer but didn't strike at her. "No." It growled and if Azy didn't know better, she'd think it was frustrated with her. "Jett comes. AllFather dies."

The table above them both disappeared, and, in its place, a very large, very angry dragon stood, ready to pounce on the demon. The demon dragon lunged and thrust the mirror at her face. Before Cage could strike, it disappeared in a puff of smoke.

Her dragon gently grabbed her up into one claw, cradling her body and holding her to his warm scales. Azy slumped into his hold, her mental and physical reserves toast. Never had she ever been so grateful to have all these friends, her true family in her life. She simply didn't know if that would be enough.

They'd won the battle today. But barely.

If Ereshkigal truly coveted the babies... a jagged tear of fear the size of the Marianas trench had been ripped open inside of her. No, Azy wouldn't give in to that fear. Even if everything in their lives had to change, if they had to give up everything, they would find a way to keep their children safe.

In a wash of golden light, Cage shifted into his human form holding Azy in his arms. "I thought he was going to kill you."

Yeah. She'd thought so too. She stretched her back trying to work on a twinge that had her lower back aching after that battle. "That's the crazy thing. He talked to me, in that way that some of the smarter demon dragons do. He said he wants to help us."

Cage looked at her like she was a crackhead on crack. She kind of felt like she'd been slipped a hallucinogen. This was one weird idea. "For real. He said if I called Jett, they would kill the AllFather, and I think they mean the Black Dragon. He said he would help save the babies from Ereshkigal."

Match threw a chair across the room. "You must never let her touch your children. It is a fate worse than death."

Cage stood, pulling her up with him, rubbing his hands over her arms, ribs and belly, checking her for injuries. "You're telling me The Black Witch wants our children and a demon dragon is proposing a deal to save them?"

She did sound like she was on drugs. Right. The rest of them had been under the witch's spell when she'd laid that evil nugget on Azy. "Pretty much."

The love of her life stared down at her, his eyes flitting back and forth over hers as if he was trying to get into her brain. He raised a hand and gently lifted her chin with his finger. "I'm not going to let either of those things happen. You and I will protect our children."

He pressed his lips to hers, sealing his promise with his kiss. It's not like Azy thought they wouldn't fight fist and claw for their family's lives, but Cage's assurances healed up a part of the fresh shreds of fear the Black Witch had torn in her soul. She swept her tongue over his lips, asking him to deepen the kiss.

"We all will." Jakob sat a few chairs over with Ciara in his lap.

At his words Cage pulled away from Azy's mouth, but ran his thumb over her lips, staring at them with a promise for later. He pulled her toward two chairs that hadn't been destroyed at the front of the room. Rays of sun shot down through the destroyed roof directly onto them, reminding Azy of the way heavenly light always shined on the throne of a king in fairy tales.

Cage sat Azy down first and then took the seat next to her. There was something new and different about him. A stronger power had settled over him. He practically glowed with it and Azy basked in his energy. The babies noticed it too. They had worn themselves out, already battling like tiny warriors.

"Thank you, Jakob. I know in the days and battles to come we will be looking to all the Wyrs for their help." Even his voice was more commanding than before. It sent a heat through her that was both arousing and comforting. "We are fortunate to have you all as our friends and family. We will be stronger together."

He pulled the sword from his belt that Azy had seen him attach to his tail during the battle. It had a familiar look, so much like the sword he used in conjunction with her mirror. "As is the way with all gifts from the First Dragon, where these came from is a mystery. But since we were each given one, with a jewel the color of our Wyr and with the symbols of our elements, I believe they are significant in our battle against the Black Death."

Cage looked to each of his Wyvern brothers, catching their eyes, some silent pledge passing between them all. It warmed her heart to see him bonding with his brothers in this new way. Even Match gave him the guy head nod.

Azy caught Ciara's eye and then Jada's. If the dragon warriors were bonding, she felt like the mates might too. Both women smiled back, and she understood they were thinking the same thing.

Jada tipped her head to the side and tapped her lips, thinking. "Where's the Black Dragon in all of this? Not that we missed him, but why wasn't he here today?"

Ky stroked his knuckles up and down Jada's arm. "I doubt he's off licking his wounds. No, he's either wreaking havoc elsewhere or planning to."

Hmm. Something important had changed and Azy was probably the only one who had the information to put the puzzle together. It made her ache to even think about the Black Witch wanting her babies. Literally pained her, low in her belly. "Ereshkigal has forsaken him."

Everyone in the room swiveled to stare at her. "It's something she said. She wants to take our children to start over. She said she needed someone who hadn't been touched by her magic. I think the her she's referring to means the White Witch."

Match paced back and forth not letting anyone stand in the way of the path he was wearing in the floor, even though Ciara was usinging her best snowflakes of calming magic to get him to sit down, calm down. "The Black Witch's powers are either growing stronger or she hasn't revealed her true strength to us if she is able to break through the protective wards. The demon dragons shouldn't have been able to even find the villa, much less enter it."

Cage took Azy's hand and squeezed. "We've never seen her in battle outside of hell. She brought the demon dragons here on her own. I'll wager a large measure of my hoard that she wreaked the destruction to The Lindens as well. Which means she's also working with Geshtianna."

A sharper pain struck Azy radiating from her back around her ribs and shooting low into her belly. Ow. Now what? God, she hoped that the streaks of white lightening the babies had generated during the battle hadn't caused them harm. She'd better get a hold of Señora Boh to come check on them after all that stress.

Cage nodded but narrowed his eyes. "Why are the Gold Dragons and the seat of our Wyr susceptible to their attacks? Jakob, you haven't seen any more demon dragons at your house?"

"Not since Ciara and I were mated. They're still in the country, but not within our protected wards."

Ciara kissed his cheek. "Do you think it's got something to do with having your soul shard stolen? Maybe the Black Witch did a spell when it was down in hell to weaken your Wyvern bond to the Wyr."

Azy grasped the shard. "No. The witch never had it. Remember, that succubus," she glanced over at Jada. The woman who'd stolen Cage's shard was her sister and was now missing. She had made mistakes but had tried at least a little to make up for them, and she was Jada's family, which meant she was important. "Portia gave the shard directly to me."

Cage growled low in his throat. "Geshtianna then. Portia was under her control when she... when I gave it to her."

"I think Ciara's on to something." Strengthen the bond. Maybe the midwife meant more than the bond between Azy and Cage needed to be fortified. The shard of Cage's soul she wore, that marked her as his mate glowed warm against her skin. "I think if we find that damn ring and get married it will help."

Cage grinned at her like a fool. "I fucking love how your brain works. I swear to you we will find your Wyvern mate's ring. We will create an unbreakable bond, you and I."

He sounded so sure, a new confidence she hadn't seen in him before. It was damn sexy.

"I know." She grabbed Cage's arm intending to give him a little squeeze, but another pain shook her. The intensity was threefold of the last one and she grabbed onto his hand hard. Ow, ow, ow. "Cage, something's wrong."

"Az? What is it?" He swooped her up into his arms and her body was wracked by stabs radiating through her so intense she cried out in pain. Cage's face lost all his color. "First Dragon help us."

"He can't help you now, dears. He doesn't know nothing 'bout birthing no babies." Señora Boh floated into the room. "Good thing you called me when you did, Azynsa."

Ow, ow, double ow. It was too soon for her to go into labor. Even if her children were growing at twice their rate, like Señora Boh said, there was no way they could be full grown. "Are the babies okay?"

Señora Boh took one look at her and signaled to Cage.

"Come. Bring your mate. Let's see if we can talk your new little warriors into staying put a bit longer."

Uh-oh. The midwife had totally avoided the question and that air of calm that she usually pervaded was uncomfortably absent. She was all business now. Not good. The aches tugging at her from the inside out were nothing compared to the one in her heart. If anything went wrong, if her babies.... well, she was going to fuck that Black Witch's life right up.

Cage shifted into his dragon form and flew out to the treehouse, their sanctuary. Señora Boh followed behind like a weird flying nun. Another sharp pain shook Azy's body just as Cage set her down in the bed. He shifted and crawled in with her, sitting behind her and wrapping his arms around her. She leaned into his chest drawing on his warmth.

He cradled her, nuzzling her neck, doing his best to keep the fear out of his own voice. Azy heard and recognized it. "My heart, I love you. No matter what. You're mine and you're going to be fine. Okay?"

More pain shot through her and she grabbed Cage's shirt, pressing her face back into his shoulder. "I'm scared, Cage."

"Now, now. There's no need to get crazy, you two. We're not going to let anything happen." The midwife crossed the room and placed her hands on Azy's belly. A white light, like the ones her babies had produced in defense against the Black Witch emanated from her hands and soaked into her skin.

The babies wiggled and a huge sense of relief washed over Azy that they were alive and kicking. It was the only thing that kept her from screaming when the next pain pulsed across her midsection. Azy gasped, the agony of it stealing her breath away. This one was the worst yet. The midwife closed her eyes, concentrating and the white light grew, surrounding them, pushing its way into her. It burned, so hot until she was covered in sweat and her vision tunneled. A ringing grew in her ears and her skin tingled like a thousand needles were skimming up and down, pricking, poking.

"Azy, hold on, baby." She could hear his frantic tone, but barely understood his words. "Stay with me. Stay, my love."

Where did he think she was going? Cage's voice disappeared into a whisper coming from someplace very far away. His arms were still around her, but his touch felt like nothing more than a feather. All she could see, hear, and feel was the light.

"Señora, save her. If she dies--"

Azy didn't hear the rest of what Cage had to say. The light was so loud, or maybe that was something else rushing through her ears. It did have a whoosh whoosh sound. Plus, that voice. Not Cage's, not Señora Boh's, yet someone she knew was calling her.

"Azynsa," the soothing voice sing-songed her name. It was so familiar, like a long lost friend. Someone she missed and hadn't seen in a long time. "Just where do you think you're going?"

Azy couldn't feel her body, didn't understand if her mouth was moving producing words or if it was her thoughts. "I, uh, I don't know. I don't want to go anywhere."

"Then don't, silly fish." The form of a beautiful woman and an extremely good-looking but fierce young man wavered on the edge of Azy's vision. "You need to help bring us back into the world."

The name calling came off more like a term of endearment from them. How did she know this couple? She certainly didn't know anything about bringing anyone back to life. She wasn't a witch, good or bad. She was just a girl from the south side of Chicago with a mermaid for a mother. "I do? I don't think you have the right person. I do know a few witches, maybe they can help."

The woman smiled and shook her head while the man remained very stoic, reminding her of Cage when they'd first met. A sadness emanated from them both. For the first time a deep male voice permeated into Azy's head. "No, you and Cage are the Gold Wyvern. You're chosen. You're the only ones who can make the hard choices to come. She's been hidden away for far too long. They can't protect her any longer and It's time for me to rejoin the battle."

Damn, she should know who these people were. The woman's identity was a smidgen out of reach, on the tip of her tongue, on the edge of her peripheral vision. There was an incredibly familiar feeling about them both. Like someone she'd known for a long time, like family. Which didn't make sense. Azy didn't understand much about families. She'd only ever had her dad. "Who are you? Do we know each other?"

That question made the woman's sad smile turn into a bright happiness and the young man glow with a colorful aura around him. "You'll see soon enough."

Together, they wrapped Azy into their soft but strong energy, like an ethereal hug. "I'm sorry we've put you through so much stress these past few months, but we had to hurry so that Ereshkigal and Jara didn't have time to sense us and figure out our plans. You've been so strong. I know you can be for just a little longer."

Whoa. Did this woman know more about what was going on than the rest of them? Maybe she could get some intel from her to bring back to Cage. Not that she understood where she was at the moment or how to get to Cage. She only knew she needed to. She'd had some other weird experiences since her life had become intertwined with the dragons and every time her bond with Cage, had pulled them through. She had no doubt, only complete faith that it would again. "Ereshkigal was just here. Did she do this to me?"

The couple's form faded a bit and they retreated. "No. We did and I'm so sorry. I promise it won't be for much longer, but you have to hold onto the Gold Wyvern, let him anchor you to the world. He's the one who can pull the Wyrs together. The combined power of all six is more than any Wyr individually. It's the only way to defeat the black magic of the witch and... the dragon."

Cage. Yes. He was her anchor. Azy pictured him in her mind and the white light surrounding her turned gold around the edges. Gold like Cage's scales. The pain in her belly started to fade until every last little twinge was gone, and Azy opened her eyes.

"Azynsa? My love. Holy shit, don't ever do that to me again." Cage looked down at her, his eyes swirling with the gold of his dragon, fear, relief, and love shining in them.

"I'm not going anywhere," she croaked out. They had work to do. Together. Some important people were coming.

Señora Boh wiped a strand of hair from her sweaty brow. There was more worry on the midwife's face than Azy expected. "Azynsa, listen to me. The babies are in distress. I need to help them get into the world, now. If I do not, they will die."

Time stopped, the air froze, and the sunlight faded from the room, but just for a second. Everything was going to be okay. "I - I think they're ready."

She touched her hand to Azy's belly again looked to both her and Cage. "Yes, they are. But they won't let me help them. Such little warriors they already are. They are each trying to protect the other, but it's keeping them from joining our world."

Azy reached out her hand and Cage caught it up immediately, lending her his strength. She met his eyes and took a deep breath, making the hard decision and trying to tell him with her calm tone that everything would be all right. "Cut me open to get them out. Babies are born by Cesarean all the time. I'll heal."

Cage growled but didn't say no. He knew they would have to make this sacrifice too.

"No, we don't need to cut you. I can bring them out with magic. But they have to allow me to do it. The two of you need to be shining lights for them. They know you, but there is a dark force in this world trying to keep them from being born and they know it."

"We will protect them." Cage snarled and gripped her even tighter in his arms. "The other Wyverns and their mates have pledged to help us. No evil will keep our children from living."

Oh, how she loved his fierce protectiveness. "Tell us what to do and we'll do it. Help us help them."

Señora Boh nodded and rubbed her hands together. She closed her eyes and the white light glowed from between her palms. "Focus all your energy, the power you yield over the elements, the light in your souls into the babies. Together you can block the darkness and I can bring them out into the light."

The witch swirled her hands and the light over Azy's belly forming an oblong ball of light, like a golden egg of magic, energy, and power. The babies moved inside of her and she squeezed Cage's hand tighter.

"I love you, Azynsa. You are my life and, "he swallowed, "while I am scared to death that there are evils out there in the world that we may not be able to keep from our children, I am so excited to have a family with you. I cannot wait to see them at your breast, watch them grow, teach them the ways of the warrior, train our first born to become the next Wyvern of the Gold Dragons."

There was so much emotion in Cage's words and Azy felt the beautifully strong power and energy he poured into them. "I never thought I would have a life like this. I'm so happy it's with you. We've already faced tough times and I'm sure there are more ahead. Where you go, I go, Cage. I love you so much."

Golden swirls of magic floated through the air around them. The babies pushed against her and Azy had never felt so safe in her life. Her babies would be okay. She and Cage had so much love and life to look forward to.

"It's not enough." Señora Boh frowned and her voice was strained. She even had sweat beading over her top lip. "We need more magic. I'm losing them."

What more could they give? She and Cage were already sharing every bit of love they had.

"Kiss me, Cage. Let me feel your love, let them." She tipped her face up to his and brushed her lips across his. This kiss wasn't filled with their normal heat, it wasn't about lust, but being together. It was so beautiful, Azy was sure she heard music.

Cage broke the kiss and rubbed his nose against hers. "Do you hear that?"

From below, down on the beach, three voices lifted up in song so beautiful it brought a tear to Azy's eyes. Her mermaid sisters were singing a lullaby. One that Azy was sure she'd heard long ago, but their voices weren't the only ones.

The Mami Wata had barely been friendly to her, but they

had taken her in. She'd never thought of them as family. Yet here stood three of them, here in their time of need.

How had she ever thought she didn't have a real family?

She'd thought it would always be just her and Cage, the two of them against the world. But it never had been.

The world hadn't been against them from the beginning. It had been conspiring for them.

Against all the odds and evils put in their paths they had found the way to each other.

At each step, each challenge the dragon warriors, the amazing women they had mated, and even the mermaids had been there to help overcome the forces trying to stand between them.

That's what a real family did. Family was a powerful force, forever. Family was forever.

Forever.

Was it? Hers hadn't been. Her mother had left her and then died before she could even know her. Her father had been killed when she was only eighteen.

Her life was completely different now and she knew the answer. For the first time in her life, she knew it in her heart. Even if her own parents weren't here now, they were always with her. Just like she would be for her children. No matter what. Forever.

"I know what to do to fill the babies lives with all the magic we need."

UNITED

Cage was sure as shit glad Azy was calm and collected because, while he was the warrior, the leader of his Wyr, and maybe more, he needed her to keep him from returning to that place of fear he'd been living in the past few months. He'd feared for her life, for the lives of every dragon in his Wyr, that he was not going to be the leader they needed to rebuild after the attacks, and deep inside, his worst fear, that he wouldn't be the kind of father his twins needed.

He'd kept all of that bottled up inside, not wanting to put the burden of those worries on her or ask his brother Wyverns for help. They'd done enough. Except already today he'd learned they were all more powerful when they worked together and shared the weight of the world and its battles with each other.

Looking down at his beautiful lover, the woman who held his soul both literally and in her heart, Cage knew he was lying to himself. His real problem lie rooted in the knowledge that Azy, the other Wyverns, his Wyr, and his children would think he wasn't fit if he was scared. So he'd hidden those worries by wrapping them up in a disguise of control. He hadn't let anyone see his dirty little secrets.

Until he'd lost his soul shard to the succubus, he'd never really needed to be a leader. His Wyr followed him because that's what they were expected to do. Not because he was some great warrior.

He wasn't trying to protect them, any of them. He'd been protecting himself. Screwing around with everyone's lives by not living up to even his own expectations of what the Gold Wyvern should be. He was such a dumbass. Azy was a better leader than he'd ever been. Today and for the rest of his life he would do his best to have courage and be the mate she deserved. Starting right now.

"Tell me what you need, mate and I will make it happen."

So much love permeated from her. "Take me down to the beach. We and our babies need our friends, our family, and our elements."

Cage immediately knew where she was going with this. Dragons and mermaids, witches and a succubus, even whatever kind of being Ciara's friend Wesley was - they all brought a special kind of magic and joined together they would be more than enough to help the babies feel safe and protected so they could come into the world. He glanced over at Señora Boh to make sure she was on the same page and she nodded to him. In the blink of a dragon's eye he shifted and carefully lifted Azy into his talons. She wrapped her arms around his foreleg and together they swooped out of the treehouse. In a long twisting glide, they were down to the beach a stone's throw from where the mermaids gathered.

The lilting song the mermaids sang drifted through the air and washed over them. As soon as he landed, Azy's sisters helped her up and guided her toward the water, surrounding her in a circle of feminine mystique. With each step she took, another mermaid's head popped up out of the ocean and joined their voices to the song. Then another, and another, and soon the water was filled with Mami Wata and their lyrical lullaby.

"Cage, I need you too." Azy waded into the softly lapping waves, not transforming her legs to her beautiful tail.

I'll be there, my love. Let me gather the dragons. We're better, stronger, and have more magic together.

She nodded and her eyes sparkled. "Yes. We need them too. Bring everyone."

Azy was happy, not worried, not fearful, but excited that they were bringing everyone together and would soon meet their children. She filled him with so much love he was overflowing with it. He jumped back into the air, did a flip in the wind and flew up to the villa. The Wyverns and a half dozen gold dragons were gathered in the destroyed dining room.

He glanced around and a warm surprise smacked him in the face. They were cleaning up and repairing the damage done in the attack. An inkling of an idea popped into his mind.

Working together. Not just right now.

Even AmberGris, his second in command was there. That surprised the shit out of him. Cage had left him in Dubai continuing the hunt for Geshtianna, his brother, and Portia.

Cage shifted and approached his friends. "Gris? What are you doing here?"

They clasped hands, greeting each other in the way of friends and compatriots. "I got here as fast as I could when I received your call. Many more will arrive tonight and tomorrow. The Wyr is here for you, Azynsa, and the new children. We will protect them."

His call? Cage had yet to ask everyone for their assistance. Something to sort out later. He hadn't gotten an update on the hunt for Geshtianna and the missing dragon warriors from their Wyr in a while. They were his second priority, right after taking care of his family. "We only have a moment. Tell me quickly. Do you have news of Gris and Portia? Of the succubus queen?"

Gris's eyes went from amber to swirling with black grief and a dangerous anger. "No. The trail we found in Dubai has gone cold. I have lost them."

Cage would not accept that. He clasped AmberGris on the arm and willed him to listen, using his Wyvern alpha's voice. "We will find them. When you have the warriors you need, form a war council. Enough of chasing our own tails. We will call an AllWyr and ask the other Wyvern's to join us in the hunt for the succubus queen and her minions."

"BUT, my lord, this is a Gold Wyr matter. Only our warriors and my mate have been kidnapped. We will take care of our own." Gris frowned and looked around at the other dragon warriors, their mates, and friends. He too wasn't used to asking for assistance from anyone. The golds had been a powerful Wyr for so long and their money kept them from ever needing much of anything.

Friendship and family weren't something one could buy. "It's time we ask for help. No amount of pride... or fear will keep us from saving your brother and mate or destroying those who have harmed us. It's time to unite."

Gris was privy to almost everything a Wyvern knew since he would have to take over the role should Cage die before he had an heir. The look of surprise on this hardened warrior would be funny at any other time. Uniting the Wyrs wasn't exactly an everyday occurrence. It wasn't even an every century event. "Yes, sir."

"All of our dragon warrior brothers will learn the value of combining our skills and forces. Here and now is the place to start." Cage knew how to do it, that wasn't the question. Would the other Wyverns agree? They hadn't ever even discussed the possibility. He jumped up on top of the large dining room table. "Wyverns, warriors, mates, and friends. Azynsa and I need your help."

The heady ring of his alpha voice pierced the air grabbing everyone's attention. His gold dragon warriors couldn't help but respond, but even Jakob, Ky, and Match looked up at him.

"Is Azy okay? The babies?" Ciara asked.

"The midwife has told us the twins are in distress and she needs to bring them now. But there is a dark force, it is the same one many of us have battled. This evil does not want these two new dragon warriors born." His statement was met with many low growls and a few gasps. Cage knew the feeling.

"I ask of you now a move that hasn't been done since the great battle for hell the First Dragon and the White Witch fought so many years ago at the dawn of the age of Dragon Warriors. We must combine our magic, our Wyrs under one banner to push back this evil."

More of his golds got that same look that Gris had, surprised their Wyvern would even suggest such a bold move. "Together, we can save my children." Cage pulled up the courage he needed to complete the first wing of his request. "Together we can help the new generation of Dragon Warriors into the world."

That sparked interest from everyone in the room. Good. He wasn't the only one who needed to think of the twins as new warriors. They were truly the first children of this generation and long overdue. There was a reason for that, even if they didn't yet know what it was. Cage knew in his heart that his boys would lead the way for the rest of the unborn souls of dragon warriors waiting to come into the world. Maybe even lead them in life and the battle for good when they were grown too.

Now that he'd planted the idea in their heads, he would drive the need to unite the Wyrs home. "If it was only the Black Dragon, we might be able to fight him off on our own as we have so far. We've sent him running and his army hiding. But Ereshkigal attacked us on her own and she is no mere witch. Only when we fought as one, did we scare her away. It won't be enough. She will be back."

His gut told him more trouble was brewing. Bringing the Wyrs together now would not only help his children safely into the world, it might be the only way to stop the rising darkness that was coming. They'd had no reason to join forces for centuries. Warrior life had become easy. A few demon dragon hunts here or there and no mates lives to worry about.

This generation of Wyverns he was a part of had all come into their Prime within a few years of each other and had all inherited their Wyrs around the same time. Each were young for accepting that mantle of responsibility, even Match who was the eldest of them all. Unlike their fathers before them, he, Ky, Jakob and Match had learned to work together like when Cage's soul shard had been stolen. But they were still completely independent of each other. That had to end. If they were going to defeat these dark foes.

"Brothers, join me. Unite our Wyrs here and now. Help my children into the world and then follow me into battle to defeat those that would bring their plague of evil to our world once and for all."

The room went completely silent, each person considering Cage sent up a prayer to the First Dragon asking for help and guidance and maybe a little luck and faith.

Ky grabbed Jada up in a heated kiss and then stepped up onto the table as the first Wyvern to either challenge or join Cage. This was the moment of truth.

"I, Kaiārahi Tarakona Puru, Wyvern of the Blue Dragons will help you, brother. I pledge the loyalty of the Blue Dragon Wyr to you and join you in this fight against evil." Ky clasped Cage's forearm and a clap of blue and gold magic shuttered through the air, sealing their fates together.

Jakob pressed his head to Ciara's, brushed his lips across hers and joined them on top of the makeshift dias. "I, Jakob Zeleny, Wyvern of the Green Dragons am here in aid to you, brother. I pledge the loyalty of the Green Dragon Wyr and its warriors to you." Jakob too extended his hand to Cage and when they shook on it another wave of magic, this time green and gold flashed through the room.

All eyes went to Match. If anyone united Dragonkind it should be the Red Wyvern, the Alpha of alphas, first son of the first son. Cage couldn't wait for Match to do it. Either they acted now, or his whole world would be destroyed.

Match jumped up on the table. He extended his arm to Cage and they clasped each other. Match looked so deep into Cage's eyes, he might as well have crawled inside his head. "I, Maciej Cervony, Wyvern of the Red Dragons will help you, your mate, and your children, brother."

Gratitude of the highest magnitude poured from every cell in Cage's body. It was more than any red dragon warrior, much less their Wyvern had ever given. The Red Wyvern was the rightful leader of the dragon warriors and it meant more than anyone could say that he was willing to allow Cage to unite the Wyrs under the Gold banner.

"But," He gripped Cage's arm even harder. "Until I find my mate, I cannot join your battle. I must save her first."

Match had a mate? Cage searched his brother Wyvern's eyes. A quick glance down at Match's neck showed his dark red soul shard still hanging there. Inside the faintest of a spark flickered.

Holy shit. Cage exchanged a look with Ky and Jakob. They were as surprised as anyone. Cranky ass bastard had been keeping secrets. Match had a mate.

"I understand." Later he was sure they would have time to ask the one million questions about who and where this mysterious mate was and how they could help find and rescue her. Because First Dragon above, they all knew Match needed to get laid. And Cage knew the love of a mate would change everything for his brother Wyvern.

The one warrior none of them would think capable of love held a deep grief in his eyes. "Still I pledge the loyalty of the Red Dragon Wyr to you. Lead them well, AllWyvern."

At his final word a thunderclap of light and heat, gold and red shook the room. It was done. They Wyrs were united for the first time in centuries, and Cage was the Wyvern of all. It was a responsibility he would hold only as long as absolutely necessary and wield with great care.

Cage looked around the room, a new sharpness to his gaze. His first order of business was to throw a mantle of protection around the area to help his twins meet their new family. "To the beach."

The dragons shifted and they all flew with the help of the wind down to the beach in only moments. They gave room for those carrying their mates to land first and shift. Cage set down right at the edge of the water and waded in to where Azy floated nearby surrounded by the mermaids. She held Señora Boh's hand, but as he approached, she reached for him instead.

She squeezed his hand and drew him close to her. "Wow. Either having babies is making me hallucinate or you're glowing."

As was the shard hanging from her neck. Cage kissed her on the forehead and sank down into the water beside her. "I'll tell you all about it later. How are you feeling? How are the babes?"

A new round of the mermaids' song lifted into the air and resonated across the water. The three who'd been visiting them the past few days swam over and guided Ciara, Jada, Fleur, and Wilhelmina into the water with them. After just a few seconds the women picked up the simple lullaby and sang along too.

"They're naughty is what they are. Wiggly and poking me in the everywhere. Still they won't let Señora Boh help them come out. They even shocked her on her last try."

Cage chuckled. "That's my boys. I have a feeling they'll be a handful the rest of our lives."

Azy rolled her eyes, but she grinned too. That smile turned into a grimace and she gripped his hand hard and buried her face in his chest, burying a groan of pain.

Señora Boh placed a hand on each of their shoulders. "We can't wait any longer. AllWyvern, call forth your dragons. We need the touch of everyone's elements to call up the magic to push back the evil hunting these babies. I need everything you've got to pull them into our world."

Cage nodded. He let a partial shift take him over, his

dragon rising just to the surface, changing only his eyes into the gold of his dragon so that he could mentally call out to the united Wyr.

Brother warriors. Call upon the gifts bestowed on you by the First Dragon and the White Witch. Give us your wind and sun, bring forth the water and ice, send us the healing power of the Earth, and reign down the fire of dragons. Let your gifts become one to share with those who need our protection.

Gold dragons flew in a circle above their heads, at first only five or six made up of a few warrior guards stationed at the villa. Within a few minutes though more dragons joined them coming from all four directions until the sky was a golden vortex. Rays of sun shined down onto Azy and Cage and a warm breeze swept over their skin. A soft greenish fog found its way onto the breeze and swirled around them. Jakob and Steele blew the healing breath that Green Dragons possessed into the air. This dragon's breath was filled with white sparkles as Ciara stopped singing and lifted her arms into the air, calling on her own gifts as a white witch.

Great walls of trees, vines, and plants that Cage couldn't even identify grew up creating a barrier between the secluded beach and the rest of the world. Several blue dragons surfaced alongside the mermaids. Ky must have called them. A gentle rain pitter-patted down onto the leaves and the waves around Cage and Azy slowed to a gentle rocking.

Match was the only red dragon present and his fire was the final element. Cage wasn't sure how the Red Wyvern would yield his power without burning the trees, filling the sky with smoke, boiling the water, or singeing everyone with his breath of fire. Their exchange of magic when Match pledged his Wyr to Cage, demonstrated that he was the most powerful red the world had ever seen and a keeper of the ancient flame. He would do the right thing.

Match shifted into his great beast of a dragon and raised his wings. He closed his eyes looking every bit the image emblazoned on the minds of the world of what a dragon represented. Slowly, lifted by the breeze, red sparks lifted up off of his back, legs, and neck, turning from glittering scales into fiery embers, a fountain of sparkling fire.

Azy gasped. "Oh my goodness. That's…he's amazing."

Indeed, he was. The embers floated on the breeze, some alighting on Cage and Azy, but instead of burning them, they soaked into their skin, giving them renewed energy. More embers joined the other elements and the riot of colors combined into a blinding beautiful white light.

"It's time." Señora Boh bowed her head and circled her hands over Azy's belly. The same golden egg-shaped ball formed between the two of them.

Azy tensed in his arms and breathed in and out fast and hard like she was running a marathon. "Cage, oh God. This does not feel good."

She groaned and suppressed a cry into his chest. He held onto her so tight and pulled his own sun and wind down to comfort her as best as he could. "You can do it, Az. I'm here for you. Everyone is here for you."

The mermaids lowered their volume until their song was almost a whisper and the only distinct voices were that of Zambezi and the dragon warriors' mates. The white magic continued to swirl around them and Señora Boh began to shake with her effort.

Azy cried out again and Cage watched horrified as the skin on her stomach rippled. "Ooooow. Holy Mary, Mother of God. Ow."

"I'm sorry, love. I wish I could do anything else to help you. Tell me what you need, Azynsa."

"Ow, ow, ow, ow. If this is how dragon babies are born, we are never having sex ever again, you big dumb dragon." She squeezed his hand hard enough to cut off his circulation.

That was just the pain talking. He hoped. "Love, I will be your devoted celibate mate the rest of my days if you wish."

"Don't be an asshole. You are sexing me up the second I feel up to it." She sneered at him and wrinkled up her nose.

"Almost. Hold on. I've almost got them." Each of Señora Boh's words came out on a grunt. She was sweating and red in the face. This process was taking a toll on her as well. "Come on, you little stinkers."

Azy's eyes went wide and Cage's stomach clenched. She squeezed her face tight and gave a great wrenching scream. The world exploded into fireworks of every color and the land and sea shook beneath them.

Azy lay limp in his arms. No. Sun and sky, no. "Azy? Azynsa. Baby, can you hear me?"

"They can hear you on the moon," she groaned.

Thank the First Dragon. Cage held her tight to him and brushed a kiss across her forehead. She opened her eyes and turned her gaze toward Señora Boh. The midwife held between her hands, in that egg of golden light, two tiny babies.

"Congratulations. You have a son... and a daughter."

A joy so intense burst from Cage's heart he thought it might explode. He was so happy, he didn't even register what the midwife had said for a moment. A son. The next Gold Wyvern.

And a daughter.

Uh. Wait a minute.

A daughter? "Señora. I think you need to check again. Dragons do not have daughters. There is no such thing as a female dragon."

The midwife floated the egg of light over to them and set it gently on Azy's chest. "They'll need to stay in the light until they are strong enough to face the world head on. A few weeks, maybe a month or so. We'll see how they grow. And I assure you, dragon or not, you do have a daughter."

Huh. "A daughter."

Azy smiled up at him and cradled the babies in their light. For all the fuss, they were fast asleep. No crying or wails, just the two cutest little babies on the face of the planet. She whispered to him. "Aren't they beautiful?"

Yes, they were. Cage gently lifted the babies and held them aloft. "We have a son and daughter!"

The dragons, mermaids, friends, and family erupted into cheers.

WHO WANTS TO GET MARRIED?

While Azy slept Cage kept watch over the incubator of light the witch had surrounded his children in. In the few short days since they'd been born they'd grown so much it was visible. Every time he looked at them, they were bigger and stronger.

He would do anything to protect them. They'd moved from the little treehouse into the main villa so there would be no more flying back and forth. A new elite guard of mixed dragons was on century duties twenty-four seven to keep watch over the children and the house.

"There's this tradition, son, that when babies are born, the father hands out cigars to all of his friends to celebrate." A warrior with a prosthetic arm stepped up beside Cage and looked down at the little egg of light.

He pulled two cigars from a pocket, and handed one over, biting off the end of the other. "My mate doesn't like these things, but I say where there's smoke, there's fire, and I am a dragon after all, so fire is a good thing." He blew a tight flame at the end of his cigar and got it burning.

Many dragons from all of the Wyrs had come through to see the new babies and pay their respects to him and Azy. There would be plenty of pomp and circumstance as the Wyrs transitioned to this new united state. So far none had challenged his status as the AllWyvern.

Cage didn't know this particular warrior by name. He was well into his Prime and with his scars had seen many battles. With the ability of dragon's fire, he was obviously a red, so Match must have brought some of the Red Wyr in to help prepare the battle strategy. Reds were ruthless in their hatred of demon dragons.

"Thank you, warrior. I appreciate the gesture." Cage took the cigar and twirled it in his fingers.

"You know, kid. Babies are tougher than they look. Yours are the toughest. Their little souls have been around the block a few times, and they are well prepared for this life. So, don't you worry about them. I've done plenty of that for you. With some love and guidance from you and your mate, they'll grow up to be fine warriors."

Warriors. He was having a hard enough time understanding that he had a daughter, much less that she would be a warrior. "I want to help them do that. How can I when all I want to do is wrap them up in fluffy clouds and never let the evils of the world know they exist?"

"I wanted to protect all my dragonlings when they were first born too. But that would have been both a bad idea for them and the world. My brood have all fought a lot of battles with a lot of demons. The Earth would have been a very different place, dark and filled with fear and death had our children not defended it." The warrior took a puff on the cigar but didn't blow out any smoke, rather he blew soft green puffs of healing dragon's breath.

"If they get hurt," if they died, he couldn't voice that thought. He had to be courageous for his children. "I don't think I could handle it."

Both men stared down at the little ones. "Somehow you do. They'll have plenty of scrapes and bruises as they grow up. Nothing prepares you for losing one though. When we lost Jara, I nearly burned the world down myself."

This man had given the greatest of sacrifices in the fight against evil. "Why didn't you?"

"My mate reminded me there were others still living in the world that I cared about. We had to go on for the rest of them. They were all hurt and mourning the loss of their brother too. Especially his sister. So, you find a way. It's not easy. It won't be for you either. You find a way to go on. Not the same as before. But you do." The elder dragon warrior clapped Cage on the back. "You don't have to worry about any of that just yet. They're not ready to go off and fight anything but the sandman. Revel in their innocence as long as you can."

Azy came in, joining the two men. "How are our kidlets this morning? Have you been up with them long? You should have woken me."

She picked up the ball of light and cradled the egg with their tiny children inside. They made the perfect picture. Except for the fact that his beautiful mate couldn't yet hold the twins in her arms, let them suckle at her breast. The midwife assured them the light took care of all their needs, drawing on the magical energy the dragons and mermaids had provided at their birth.

"You needed your rest, love." He ran a hand over her hair, tucking a lock behind her ear. He turned to introduce Azy to the warrior, but the man was gone. His words remained in Cage's mind for him to mull over later.

Azy leaned into Cage and hummed the mermaid lullaby to them. Her voice was so soft and sweet. Alluring. At the end of the song, she set them back down in the bassinet and stared at them. "I know Señora Boh said they are out of danger, that Ereshkigal can't find them in the light and when they are fully grown, they won't need that protection anymore. I'm still so worried about them. What if the demon dragons show up again? I can't protect them the same as I could when they were still growing inside of me."

Cage's chest contracted, feeling every bit of Azy's worry. He would be strong for her. "We've reinforced the wards and more dragon warriors are arriving every hour. The villa and the surrounding area are in total lockdown. Nothing is getting in. But there is one more thing we can do."

An unbreakable bond. He and Azy already had that. Perhaps the rest of the world needed to know it was true.

He bent down on one knee and took her hands in his. "Azynsa, I know we're already planning a wedding, but I've never asked you. Will you marry me? I want the whole world to know you're the light of my soul, the mate of my heart. I know we don't yet have the Wyvern mate's ring, but the human ritual has a magic of its own and--"

Azy looked down at him with more love in her eyes than he ever deserved. But he was greedy and would hoard all of it for himself. "You sweet, silly dragon. You don't have to convince me, you know."

This would be better if he did have a ring for her. He should have made her one. "I was trying to be romantic. I know our relationship hasn't had the traditional path. I thought I'd try to do this one thing right."

She pulled him up and wrapped her arms around him. "You've done a million things right. Our romance is different than anyone else's. I wouldn't have it any other way. I love you so very much."

Cage wanted nothing more than to make love to his mate, but she had just birthed twins a few days ago, so he would be content to hold her in his arms for now. Azy reached down and squeezed his butt. Naughty mermaid. He squeezed hers in return, but chastely turned them both, throwing his arm over her shoulder and guided her wandering hand around his waist.

Her fingers wandered anyway and reached into his pocket. "Cage? What's this?"

She pulled out a ring, glowing like pure sunshine. They both stared at it the light reflecting in each other's eyes.

"Holy First Dragon. You found it. You found your ring." Pride swelled inside of him at his clever, clever mate.

"Have you been hiding it in your pocket all this time?" Her voice was filled with wonder as she stared at the precious item. The one last thing they needed to prove to the world that she was his true mate.

"I-I don't-" A flash of fuzzy memory shot through his mind. Trying to make her a ring, failing, another dragon helping him. Creating the swords. "Maybe I have. I think the First Dragon may have been involved in this."

"I thought the White Witch had to hide it for me."

"I'm not the one who put it in my pocket for you to just find." Cage chuckled.

Azy smacked him on the arm and then pulled him down for a tail-tingling kiss. "Let's get married right away. I know Ciara's had everything planned forever. I saw her files. She's been planning a wedding like this since she was a little girl. I kind of think she pulled together all the elements of how she wanted to get married."

Azy chewed on the side of her lip, thinking up something devious, Cage could tell. "You know I don't really care about the ceremony that much, as long as I'm there with you, the details don't matter. What would you think if we asked Jakob and Ciara to join us? If we got married at the same time?"

"You would share your wedding day with her?"

"She's my friend. It would make the whole thing a real celebration of love." A pretty pink flushed took over Azy's cheeks when she said the words.

Cage had never heard her call anyone a friend before and he wasn't sure she ever had. "Then we can certainly go ask them."

They gathered up the babies and walked down the hall to the Green Dragon guest room flanked by a gold and a red dragon warrior. Vines were crawling all up and down the door. Cage knocked and they didn't wait long until Jakob, wearing green silk pajama pants and very mussed hair answered. Well, more stood there staring at them, than anything else.

The rustling of bed coverings came from behind the door. "Jakey-poo come back to bed."

Jakob got a sloppy grin on his face. "I'm being beckoned so unless there's a battle brewing..."

His tone indicated that they should hurry to deliver their message and get out because he had very important things to attend to. Cage cleared his throat to explain but didn't have to. Azy shifted the babies to her hip and held up her hand with the ring. "I thought Ciara might like to see my wedding ring."

A squeal sounded from inside and soon the door was jerked the rest of the way open. Ciara, wrapped in a green bedsheet reached out her hand for Azy and yanked her into the room, although was careful of the babies in Azy's arm. "Let me see, let me see."

The ladies went into full on girly mode, their voices going up in pitch and volume as Azy explained how she'd found the ring. Jakob ushered Cage inside too. "You know Ciara is going to push Azy to get married right away now, right?"

"That's the plan actually. But I'd better warn you, she wants you and Ciara to share the wedding with us, get married at the same time."

Jakob blinked and then ran a hand through his hair. "That's totally up to Ci. She's the one dragging her feet. I told her we could have a wedding any time she wanted. She maintains we had one when we did the mating ceremony. She's still pretty mad about it too."

"Jakob Zeleny. That is not why we haven't gotten married." Ciara sat on a small couch next to Azy. Several flowers nearby wilted.

Azy shot Cage an uh-oh look. Yeah. Maybe the two of them should leave and let Jakob and Ciara have at it. Cage didn't want any lovers' spats to ruin Azy's happy glow. It was a nice thought she'd had to include their friends, but these two maybe weren't ready for that.

Azy touched Ciara on the arm. "I'm sorry if this started a fight between you. I meant it to be about love."

Ciara patted Azy's hand. "No. It's okay. I really appreciate the gesture. I guess Jake and I still have some things to work out. Like why he hasn't asked me to marry him."

Yikes. Lightening flashed across the ceiling. Ciara was a white witch and had many powers, weather being one of them.

"Wait. What? What do you mean I haven't asked you? I told you we could have a wedding at least a dozen times."

"But you didn't once ask me to marry you, you big dumb lizard."

Cage elbowed Jakob in the ribs. "Mates like it when you're romantic, little brother."

"Is that it? You've been waiting for me to ask you?"

Wind whipped through Ciara's hair. "Yes."

A couple more doors in the hallway opened at the commotion. Ky stuck his head into the open doorway to the Green Dragon room. "What's going on in here, bro?"

Jada slipped under his arm and tugged Ky with her to gather near Azy. She immediately lifted Azy's hand with the ring and then winked at her. In another moment, Steele and Fleur had joined them as well.

"First Dragon above. I thought it had something to do with your mother. I know how much a wedding means to you." Then he whispered under his breath, "now, anyway."

Ciara stood from the couch and stomped over to Jakob. Little storm clouds floated across the room and crackled over Jakob's head. Snowflakes dropped out of the bottom of the dark clouds. Cage side-stepped them and joined Azy ready to swoop her up should Ciara's weather get anymore wound up.

Wesley walked in a second later, took in the scene and plopped down on the couch. "Did I miss anything good?"

Jada whispered to him. "Azy found her ring and Ciara's mad because Jakob hasn't asked her to marry him."

"Ciara, dear. What is going on in here? It's so early and I need my beauty sleep." Wilhelmina walked into the room looking like she'd been up for hours doing her hair and makeup, except for the yellow satin men's pajamas she had on.

"Mina. Stay out of their business and come back to bed." A gold dragon warrior, a few decades older than Cage but still in his Prime named Auric Mosely sauntered in, naked as the day he was born. He nodded at Cage. "My lord. Congratulations on the birth of your children."

"Ooh. I hope somebody brought popcorn," Wes said.

Ciara spared a glance at her mother, and a double take at the naked warrior, but her focus was one-hundred percent for Jakob. "I know you don't get human customs, but this one is important to me. I... thought you'd--"

"*Miláčku*--" Jakob crooned.

Ciara wagged her finger at him. "Don't you *miláčku* me."

"What's milk achoo?" Wes whispered.

"*Miláček* is a term of endearment in Czech," Jada whispered back. Leave it to a succubus to know how to say sweetheart in multiple languages.

Jakob glanced over at the gathering of people and blew out a long breath. "I was waiting for our wedding to give you this but seems like I fucked that up."

He waved his hand and a leafy vine snaked across the floor and a flower bloomed. Sitting inside the petals was a small velvet box. Jakob grabbed it and sank down onto one knee, just as Cage had only an hour before. "I've been reading up on your wedding customs, *miláčku*, because I know how much they mean to you. I swear I thought that since we were already mated, I didn't need to ask you to marry me. I'm very sorry I was wrong about that."

Ciara sucked in a breath to say something. Jakob stopped her, taking her hand and opening the ring box. "I got this for you because I read in one of your wedding magazines about matching wedding band sets. You've got your ring already, and I thought this one would go nicely with it."

A large green emerald threw sparkles across the room. Or maybe that light was from Jakob's soul shard glowing on Ciara's neck. "Oh, Jakob."

"Ciara, love of my life, mate of my soul, will you marry me...today?"

"Today? Wilhelmina squeaked.

"Yes, yes, a thousand times, yes."

The group of them sitting on the couches clapped and gave hoots and hollers. Wes stood and stretched. "I guess we're having some weddings today then. Better get to work. Anyone else want to get married while we're at it?"

Auric cleared his throat. "What do you say, Mina? Want to marry me again?"

A golden glow grew from the soul shard at Auric's throat. He slipped the talisman over his head and placed it gently around Wilhelmina's neck. She sniffed and touched the shard. "About time you asked me that, you fool."

"Mother? How do you know this naked man?"

"He's the old friend who invited me here, Ciara. Honestly. Pay attention. Also, we were lovers once, and he's your father."

Ciara gaped and for the first time in as long as he'd known her, she was completely speechless. Cage knew the feeling. If Auric was her father, Cage wasn't the only dragon who had a daughter. Ciara was no dragon though. Could that possibly mean his little girl wouldn't have to be a dragon warrior either?

Azy gripped his hand and shot him a look. She was thinking the same thing as he.

FOUR WEDDINGS AND A...

At sunrise the next morning, Azy stared down the beach at the group of Wyverns who stood near the water's edge. The sun was just beginning to peak up from the horizon and it decorated the sky in streaks of gold better than any ornaments hung in a church or hall.

The men were all so handsome dressed in their dark suits, with ties and hankies to match their Wyr colors. Cage was the one she couldn't keep her eyes off of. He stood under an arch of live plants and flowers Fleur made for the occasion, saying something to the other men. When he threw his head back and laughed, it took her breath away.

Since he'd taken over the mantle of AllWyvern over the united Wyrs and the children had been born, he was different. For the first time Azy felt like she was seeing the real Cage. His worries hadn't lifted, in fact, he had a whole lot more responsibility than ever before. But his new demeanor, the quiet confidence he had now was sexy as hell and comforting in a way she hadn't expected.

"God, they are so hot in formal wear. Makes me want to

tear that suit right off and have my way with him." Ciara only had eyes for Jakob.

Wilhelmina snorted. "There will be plenty of time for that during your honeymoon. Now that you two are not living in sin."

"Mother. I told you we were not going on a honeymoon. There's a war on and we'll be busy saving the world."

"You absolutely are going on a honeymoon. It's tradition and I will--." Wilhelmina's tirade was cut off by Auric spinning her around and kissing her soundly, passionately, eye-scorchingly.

Ciara covered her eyes and reached for Azy's hand. "Oh geez. I can't watch. Tell me when it's over."

A little ping of sadness that her own parents weren't here for her wedding hit Azy behind the eyes. They were watching her from wherever they were. She had her mother's mirror tucked into a specially sewn pocket in the billows of the skirt, and her something blue was a patch from her father's Chicago police department uniform. One of the only bits of her old life as a boring teenage human girl she still had.

Azy laughed at her friend and patted her hand. "Don't look yet, Ciara. You'll burn your retinas with the heat those two are producing."

"Gah. Don't say things like that. I've had more than enough of my parents' gross PDA."

"At least your father has clothes on." Barely. Auric had agreed to a formal kilt for the occasion, but he'd made sure everyone knew there was nothing on underneath.

It took another minute, but Auric finally broke the kiss leaving a slightly dazed mother of the bride staring lovingly up at him. "Mina. Let her be. She's a strong, intelligent woman, a Wyvern's mate and a white witch to boot. You don't need to try to control her life. She's got it handled."

"Thanks, dad." Ciara said the words as a barb aimed at her mother. There was a lot of old wounds for the three of them to work on healing.

Azy had a feeling today's wedding festivities would help. This ceremony was mostly for Ciara anyway. That made Azy happier than if it had all been for her and Cage.

Wesley bustled over checking his watch, also as handsome as the devil in his suit. "All right ladies, family drama aside for the next few minutes, because it's time to get married."

He took Auric and Wilhelmina by the arm and sent them up the aisle. They were joining in the invitation and getting married today too. Then Wes held out his elbow to Ciara. "Shall we, my beauty?"

Azy stayed a moment longer and watched her friend being escorted toward her bridegroom. The flowers over the arch all came into bloom in one poof. She couldn't see Ciara's expression, only the back of the beautiful white gown that sparkled like diamonds when she walked, but Jakob's love for his mate was so very evident.

When Ciara was in his arms, that was Azy's cue. She took anxious steps toward the arch and her mate. It helped when she spotted the midwife sitting in the very front row with the children, still in their egg of light, watching along with everyone else, including their full set of guards.

Being the center of attention was so not her thing and every eye was on her. She had the urge to smooth the satiny gown she wore. Wesley had assured her this was the dress to say yes too, it's palest of rose and gold colors setting off her dark skin making her a glowing bride. She did feel pretty.

Even prettier when she caught Cage's gaze. At that very

same moment the sun burst over the horizon, sending a riot of color and heavenly rays of light through the sky. The guests gasped at the beautiful display, but she and Cage never took their eyes off each other. In this mass of people, they were the only two.

She reached Cage and took his hand. "You look ravishing, Az. I am a lucky man to have you for a mate."

A giggle bubbled up from her, letting out a little of the joy she was holding in her heart. "You're looking pretty stud muffiny yourself. I'm glad we didn't decide to run off to Vegas after all."

The priest Señora Boh had helped them find to perform the ceremony cleared his throat. He reminded Azy of a wild and extra hot Jason Mamoa, but with a prosthetic arm and a turned around collar. "Ready, my children?"

"Yes," she answered. "Bring on the love fest, padre."

The ceremony was a blur of Do-you's and I-Do's and some You-may-kiss-the-brides. Then cheering. Azy spent all her energy and attention focused on Cage and he on her. That was all that really mattered to her.

After the kissing, the priest stepped aside, and Match came out of the line of groomsmen and took the place directing the ceremony. He was a scowly as usual, until he glanced down at Azy. Then his face relaxed and he smiled that movie-star smile he had at her. "Do you have the ring?"

They purposely skipped the with-this-ring during the main part of the wedding. Even after just an evening of wearing the little bit of sunshine on her finger, she felt bare without it. She was more excited for this mating ceremony than the rest of the wedding anyway. God, she hoped that performing the ritual would truly demonstrate their bond to the whatever powers that be.

"Here you go." Ky, who was sort of serving as everyone's best man stepped up and handed Cage the ring.

The dragon warriors moved in, circling her and Cage, cutting off the view of them from the rest of the guest. Señora Boh came and stood beside them in the circle too, as if to let the babies be a part of and watch this more private part of the ceremony.

Cage retrieved a very old looking book from AmberGris and handed it and the ring over to Match. He nodded to Jakob and Ky, who took up on either side of her and Cage. Match flipped the book open and began reciting words that sounded vaguely Middle Eastern to her. She didn't understand any of them except when he said her name and then Cage's. Cage responded in the same language as if he had been asked a question and said her name.

Then both Cage and Match looked at her like she had something to say. Match rolled his eyes. She stuck out her tongue at him.

Cage chuckled, grabbed her hands and said, "Repeat after me."

She nodded and listened close to the foreign syllables so that she could say them back to him.

"Ni, Azynsa cad men anna ni gud Cage Gylden." The cadence of the sentence felt oddly familiar. She'd heard something similar to it before, but she couldn't quite put her finger on when or where. It wasn't like she spoke any foreign languages, if you didn't count mermaid.

She repeated as much as she could back to him. "Ni, Azynsa, cad men…"

"cad men anna ni gud –" Cage prompted her.

"cad men anna ni gud Cage Gylden." As she finished the sentence, Cage picked the ring up off the book Match was holding and slid it on her finger. It glowed with a light that matched the soul shard hanging around her neck, both flashing with magic.

The magic crackled through the air and a sound like shattering glass came from the protective barrier around the babies. Light streamed from cracks that spread across the shell and one teeny tiny hand of their son thrust its way through, like a little power fist bursting the bubble of magic. The light fell away in chunks, dissipating into the air and the babies lay in Señora Boh's arms, hugging each other close.

A pressure like she'd been holding her breath too long and finally let go released Azy from its tight grip. Her babies. They were here and safe and perfect. She and Cage both stared for what was only a single blink but felt like an eternity. This was their first real glimpse of their children, no barriers, no magic, only thriving amazing life.

Azy picked them both up and held them in her arms, tears streaming down her face with more joy than she'd ever known before. Their little boy had golden brown skin, a dusting of blond kinky curls, and blinked fiery eyes swirling with gold flames up at them. Their baby girl was a beautiful creamy light brown with pure white hair and eyes like frost on a winter morning.

Cage surrounded all three of them with his arms, holding them gently to his chest. "My love, they are beautiful, just like you."

"They are the most beautiful thing I've ever seen." So sweet, so precious.

"Señora?" She'd like to have the midwife check them over, make sure everything was okay. The children were so tiny, but they seemed to be fully grown. Both the midwife and the priest were gone. Like they'd simply vanished into the air. "Where did she go?"

A woman's voice came from behind Match's back. "Her job is done. She must have decided it was safe for you and your children. It is her way to leave new mothers in peace."

The warriors parted and Ninsy stepped into the circle. "She's asked me to come to help with the young warriors. I am here to serve you, my lady."

Before Azy could even acknowledge Ninsy, Match was on her in a flash. He growled low. "Where is Fallyn?"

Ninsy didn't flinch. "My service to her is through, my lord. She's off finding her way in the world."

"Exposed?" Not only smoke, but little wisps of flame licked at his lips.

Ninsy nodded, calm and serene. "She is ready."

Match stumbled back at those words, like she'd hit him with a baseball bat to the chest. He glanced around the circle of warriors and their mates, his eyes wild. "Cage, I must take my leave of you. My second in command, Brand, is ready to do whatever you need."

Cage grasped Match's arm in a warrior's embrace. "Go. Seek your revenge."

Red light, flames, shimmered over Match and his dragon burst forth, knocking over the wedding arch. He took to the sky and Cage made a motion to some of his golds to flank him. "Use the winds to help him on his journey."

Azy had about a million and a half questions, especially about her friend Fallyn. But every one of them could wait. She had her family to tend to first.

Yes. Her family. A husband, two children, and a lot of love. She could barely believe that was her life. More prickles of tears tickled her lashes and eyes. Happiness didn't even begin to describe how she felt. "Thank you for coming, Ninsy. I'm sure we'll be glad for your help soon, but not just yet."

"I understand, my lady. Please, celebrate the birth of your children, your nuptials, and the Gold Wyr's united bond. I will be at your disposal." She turned at greeted the other Wyverns with a nod to them each, then took up Wilhelmina's hand. "It is good to see you again, my friend. I am glad to have you back in our midst."

Wilhelmina shook Ninsy's hand but placed her other hand over her throat and twirled the pearls there, fidgeting with them. "Oh, I, well. It's nice to see you too."

Storm clouds formed above Ciara's head. "Mother? How do you know Ninsy?"

"She was your nanny when you were little, dear. She helped me out with you after your father left." Wilhelmina's eyes darted from Auric to Ninsy to Ciara and back again.

Ninsy didn't look old enough to Azy to have been Ciara's nanny. Then again, they didn't know what sort of being she was. It was enough for Azy to know that Ninsy had battled with the dragons before and had helped Fallyn who had been batshit crazy the last time they were together. She had a warm comforting presence and could wield a sword like a mother fucker. Sounded like perfect nanny material.

Ciara threw up her hands and walked away muttering something about way too many secrets. Jakob gave his mother-in-law a look that had Azy kind of glad she didn't have in-laws to deal with. He followed Ciara and stopped her only a couple of feet away, soothing her until her storm clouds turned into soft snowflakes and dissipated in the warm Spanish morning.

Ninsy laughed. "You know that's not how it happened. You've got a lot of explaining to do to her, don't you?"

Wilhelmina sputtered. "I-well, she, I--Ciara has been my number one priority since I knew I was pregnant."

"Mrs. Willingham?" Azy couldn't quite bring herself to call Ciara's mother by her first name. She certainly didn't feel qualified to give motherly advice. She'd only been a mom for a few days now. But she did understand what it was like not to have a mother around to share that special bond. Azy looked down at her own daughter. "She just wants to know you love her."

Auric turned Wilhelmina toward him. "It might help if you told her our story."

These guys were better than reality TV. Real Housewives of Dragon Warriors. Azy snuggled into Cage's warm chest and wondered just how much of this drama the wedding guests were seeing. If she'd been sitting there waiting, she'd have declared it was reception time already.

"I have been asking you for twenty some odd years to be my companion. Now that the Gold Wyvern has found his mate, you can finally mate your own dragon. We're a little late, but we can still be a family. Will you finally allow me to mark and claim you, Mina? It might help."

Ciara poked her head back into the circle. "Yeah, mom."

"You're sure Ciara is safe now?" Wilhelmina glanced over at her daughter, back to Auric, and then at the sleeping babies in Azy's arms.

Auric nodded and Ciara frowned. She looked like she was about to harangue her mother with a billion more questions, but Jakob hauled her back and ran his hands up and down her arms. "She is safe with me, Wilhelmina. I swear it is so."

"Well, okay. Fine then." She looked up into Azy's eyes. "You'll see soon enough, that you'll do anything for your children. Even if it means giving up your own life for them. Even if they hate you for it."

"I don't hate you, mother."

Azy would give her life for her little ones. She'd try really hard to build a solid relationship with them, so they always knew they were loved.

"It's okay. Ninsy is right. I do have a lot of explaining to do. I want to do it with your father there by my side." Wilhelmina tipped her head to the side and rolled her eyes, but she also smiled. "Do your biting thing then."

Auric laughed and swooped her up into a twirl and kissed her, giving them all a show as his kilt floated up like a schoolgirl's skirt. He set his bride down at their protests and bent his head to Wilhelmina's throat. "I claim you, Wilhelmina, as my mate. Wear my mark for all the world to see." He scraped his teeth across her skin and bit into the tender flesh there. He marked her, claimed her, and before everyone's eyes the white hair on Wilhelmina's head turned a deep golden brown, her skin smoothed, and her eyes had a whole new sparkle to them. The motherly figure now looked only a few years older than her daughter.

Azy gasped and looked up at Cage. "Uh. What just happened? Does that dragon have power over time or something?"

Ninsy laughed. "No silly. Auric is in his Prime and will be for several hundred more years. Wilhelmina's body has just adjusted to match his age. All dragons and mates do. We wouldn't want anyone widowed, now would we. That's just a terrible business. My mistress would never allow it."

Whoa. All the dragons near enough to hear Ninsy went wide-eyed. Apparently, this was news to them as well. Azy didn't even know how old Cage was or how long dragons lived. She wouldn't mind having a good long life with him. "I didn't feel a change. Are you sure?"

"Your human age is near enough to your mate that your shift is subtle."

Phew. "Cage? How old are you, honey?"

Their little boy started to wiggle and fuss. Cage stroked the boy's head and then slipped his finger into his son's grasp. "I'm a good thirty years into my prime. A hundred and eighty-one, love. How old did you think I was?"

Holy crap. He was almost nine times her age. Pervy old man. "Like, actually thirty. I thought all the Wyvern's were give or take."

He shrugged. "Essentially that's about right for human years, I guess. It's about six to one until we're around two-hundred or so. Then we don't physically age again until we're into our Wisdom years."

Oh man. If they were going to continue this conversation, she needed a drink. Granted it would be a non-alcoholic one now that the babies were here, and she was planning on breast-feeding. "I think it's time to get this party started. This is a whole lot of revelations for one wedding ceremony. We've been standing up here forever."

"Now you're speaking my language, bro." Ky raised his hands up into the air and hollered for everyone there to hear. "Let's eat cake!"

The guests cheered and clapped for the happy couples. Jada, who had of course made the cake, rolled her eyes at him. Everyone moved toward the big white tents where the wedding breakfast was set up. Azy could say one thing. Dragons knew how to par-tay.

She'd seen them fight hard, now was the time to play hard. There was dancing, and fire spitting contests, and Cage won several consecutive loopty-loop contests. The babies were oohed and ahhed over until everyone was exhausted.

Azy was sure she'd want to spend every second with her newborns but after the first very long day, she was grateful when Ninsy took them and settled them into their bassinet with the same mermaid lullaby they'd been born to.

Cage lay stretched out on their bed, his arms over his head and already snoring softly. She crawled in with him and set her head on his shoulder.

"How was your wedding day, love?" He wrapped an arm around her and rubbed a slow hand up and down her side.

"I thought you were asleep." She wasn't sure either of them were actually up to a wedding night. That was okay, they had the rest of their very long lives together to make love. "It was so much better than I ever thought I would have."

"Good. This is a day I will hold deep in my heart whenever I'm away from you." They both knew in the coming days that would be more often than they'd like. Gris had already left earlier this afternoon to head back to the search for Geshtianna.

"Hey Cage, what age do the babies start learning to shift?" There were just not a whole lot of dragon mothers around to ask this kind of stuff. Hopefully Ninsy would be knowledgeable.

"Hmm. Somewhere between forty to sixty. It's different for everyone. They'll begin warrior training at puberty. Around a hundred."

Ah, sea slug shit. "You mean they're going to be little kids until they're over sixty?"

Cage laughed. Well, he wouldn't be laughing when he was the one up changing dirty diapers at two in the morning.

She'd make sure Ninsy was not available for the stinkiest and dirtiest.

"Little kids for a hundred years." She poked him in the chest. "We are never having sex again."

"We'll see about that, baby. You're very irresistible and I'll do my best to tempt you." Cage rolled over and pinned her under him. He dotted her face with kisses, then moved down her throat and scraped his teeth over the golden mark of the dragon on her skin. She pushed her hands into his hair, encouraging him as he moved his nips and suckles down her body until she was all hot and bothered, calling his name.

Okay, no sex...except maybe tonight, and tomorrow, the night after that, and as many sultry nights as she could get with her true mate, the love of her life.

EPILOGUE: SOMEBODY HAS TO SAVE THE WORLD

In the days following Cage and Azy used the mirror and sword to search for Jett to see if there really was something, he could do to help keep the babies safe from Ereshkigal. But with no luck.

After another attempt, searching in America of all places, Cage paced around the room. "It's like that little fucker has disappeared off the face of the earth. I'm sending more warriors abroad to see if they can dig him out."

"Can we afford some of the guards? I don't want to lose any of them because what if the demon dragons find a way back in? But even I can tell those poor warriors are bored out of their minds on babysitting duty."

Ninsy came in with a baby in each arm and handed their little girl to Azy, time for a feeding. "I assure you, my lord and lady, the Gold Wyr bond you have created to the land and the people is more than enough to keep demon dragons out."

Cage lifted their son to his shoulder and patted him softly on his back. They'd continued growing and no longer looked like tiny newborns. "But we don't know the full extent of the

Black Witch's power and the Black Dragon may be nursing his wounds, but he too will be back."

The little boy started to cry, not wanting to wait his turn to eat. "Ooh, sorry there, little man. Don't cry. Everything will be just fine. Save those wails for your mommy."

"What? No. I don't think so." If she didn't have a baby trying hard to latch on, she'd flip him off.

Cage continued to croon to the child. "Oh, yes. You tell your mama you're so mad because she can't decide on a name. That's right. It's all her fault you're a poor nameless slob."

"Oh my God. Not this again. I'm not calling your daughter Goldie and her brother Locks."

"What's that, Locks? You think your mama's being stubborn. Oh, yes. Me too. But if you have a better suggestion for a name worthy of the future Wyvern of the Gold Dragons, you'd better tell her."

The little boy wailed again, clearly not having half as much fun as his father. "Yes, little boy, yes. I think that's a great idea. See if you can convince her that your name should be Apollo."

Names and their meanings or history were very important to Cage and his ancestors. Being named after the sun god was exactly the right kind of name for his first-born son. Plus, it was absolutely adorable. No brainer.

She gave Cage a big grin. "Does Apollo have any suggestions for his sister?"

Apollo screeched, which in the next breath turned to hiccups. "I don't think he does. Babe, I'm going to take him for a little flight. Have some guy bonding time while he's waiting for his turn."

In a flash Cage was in his dragon form flying out the skylight with Apollo cupped in his great talons. Their baby girl fell asleep while eating her fill and Azy got up to set her in the bassinet. Azy twirled the little sun and moon mobile hanging over the top. A shimmer of light flashed up on the ceiling and danced around the room. She spun around. Her magic mirror was glowing like it did when she and Cage used it to transport themselves through but in conjunction with the sword.

Crap. Could Cage and Apollo be in trouble?

The next instant Fallyn, dressed like a biker chick in leather pants and vest, appeared from through the reflection. She didn't even look at Azy. Without saying a word, she crossed the room and stood next to the sleeping baby looking down at her adoringly.

As soon as Azy's heart crawled back in her chest she slowly approached her long lost friend. The last time they were together, Fallyn had been very ill. Mentally unstable. Being raised in hell by the Black Dragon would do that to a person. But Ninsy had said she was better, implied Fallyn was ready to be on her own. Then there was the whole Match seeking his revenge thing. She had stabbed him in the heart with a poisoned dagger.

It probably wasn't safe for her to be here, yet Azy's gut told her she and the baby weren't in any danger. Even in her darkest days, Fallyn had a moral compass, had sacrificed to save Azy from being horribly whipped. They were tied together by a bond having come from saving each other that others would never understand. And Azy had felt connected to this woman since the day they'd come across each other in hell. She still held a deep responsibility for her that was almost as strong as the one she felt for her children. "Fallyn? Where did you come from?"

What she really wanted to ask was where she'd been. Ninsy assured them she was taking care of Fallyn, helping her to get healthy, but they had disappeared, and no one had heard from them or had even been able to find them in months.

Fallyn pulled something shiny from her pocket and hung it from the mobile on a red satin ribbon. "Hello, Izzy."

Uh-oh. This had happened when they were in hell too. At first Azy had thought Fallyn was mispronouncing her name. Turned out she was talking to someone in her head. So Ninsy hadn't been a hundred percent right about her recovery. Fallyn was still hearing voices.

Azy approached slowly and cautiously until she stood right next to the bassinet. "Izzy's not here, Fallyn. It's me your friend, Azynsa, and this is my daughter."

Fallyn ignored her all together. She picked up the baby and cradled her so gently, rocking her sweetly and cooing to her. "I wondered where you'd gone. It's quiet without you, and there are so many others lost to the dragons, I can hear my own thoughts now. How will I get by without you guiding me?"

The baby awoke and stared up at Fallyn. She didn't cry or wriggle, simply stared. The two of them were quiet for a long moment, the room still as if time had stopped. It started again when the little girl yawned and closed her eyes, making adorable sucking motions with her lips.

"You haven't named her, and she wants you to now that her brother has his." Fallyn kept her voice very quiet.

Azy swallowed. "She talked to you?"

"Not exactly. I can't hear her anymore. That was more like a thought she wanted me to have. Even this new to the world again, she is very powerful." Fallyn laid the baby back in the bassinet and pulled the blanket up to her chin. "Her name is Izzy, in case you didn't already know."

"Umm, okay." Conversations with Fallyn were always so strange. "I've always liked names like Isabelle and Isolde."

She carefully touched the gift hanging over her daughter's head, examining it. It was a gold etched star that read - Baby's First Christmas. "I'll run that one by Cage."

Fallyn stepped away from the bassinet and back over to the mirror. She touched the red necklace at her throat. "I have to go. He's looking for me. I won't be captured by him."

Why were Match and Fallyn such dire enemies? "Please stay. I'll talk to Match, make him understand. I won't let him hurt you."

"No. You can't save me again, Azynsa. Only I can."

A ping of regret poked at Azy's heart. That was the most coherent statement of conviction Azy had ever heard. Maybe Fallyn was better. "I'll help you however I can, then."

"You'll have more than enough to do. You have to find Jett." Fallyn shook her head and wrinkled up her nose, eyes scrunched tight. She swatted the air like she was trying to get rid of an annoying bug flying around her head. "Rrgh. I can't hear her. I know he needs her but she's hidden."

The moments of Fallyn's clarity must be over. Shit. This was no time for her to disappear and be on her own. "Stay here and help me find him."

Fallyn opened her eyes again and they were glowing with a red flame. She pointed to the baby. "Find Jett. She needs an army."

Azy's heart jumped into her throat like it was on a damned trampoline. "To keep her safe from Ereshkigal?"

"No. Izzy is going to save the world," Fallyn said, then touched the mirror and disappeared.

Azy sat there blinking until a moment later when Cage

swooped into the room, gently set Apollo in with Izzy, and shifted back to his handsome human form.

He quickly assessed the room. "Mate. What's happened? Match is on his way here and he's flipping his shit. Are you and the babies okay?"

She ran to him and hugged him so tight she almost couldn't breathe. He stroked her hair, calming her like no other could. When her heart slowed and she could think again, she kissed him gently. "What do you think of the name Isolda?"

KEEP READING MORE adventures with the dragons in the next full length book in the series - Defy Me.

KEEP READING for a letter from me, the author, for you, the reader, about what's coming next in the Dragons Love Curves series.

A LETTER FROM THE AUTHOR - WHO LOVES DRAGONS?

Dear reader,

I hope you loved reading this adventure in the Dragons Love Curves series with Cage and Azynsa! This story was originally supposed to be a silly little short story about how little kids are the ultimate cockblockers.

I may still write that one just for fun, but as I got into this book so many new revelations popped up and I knew it had to become a very important installment in the series.

Sometimes the dragons and their mates (and their children) surprise even me.

The dragons and their mates have a lot more adventures coming your way. So many questions to be answered.

I've got some fun surprises coming in the next books in the Dragons Love Curves series, so be sure to follow me on Amazon, Bookbub, Facebook, or my Curvy Connection to find out what happens next (hint: Jett, who doesn't have a soul shard and has decided he doesn't need one anyway is in for one wild ride.)

Stay tuned to get your fix of sexy dragon shifters giving their mates happy ever afters (and happy endings! Lol)

Keep reading for an excerpt from Defy Me, the next book in the series.

I'd love if you left a review for this story. I really appreciate you telling other readers what you thought and how the book made you FEEL!

Even if you're not sure what to say – it can be as simple as – "Read this in one sitting." or "Hooray for curvy girls and dragons." Just one sentence will do a lot.

Do you need more curvy girls getting their happy ever afters?

Want to be the first to know when the next book comes out (plus get cool exclusive content from me!)? Sign up for my Curvy Connection mailing list. Go here http://geni.us/CurvyConnection to sign up and I'll send you another curvy girl romance right away to say thanks for joining me!

Find me at www.AidyAward.com or on Facebook, Twitter, Instagram, or follow me on BookBub.

Kisses,

~Aidy

AN EXCERPT FROM DEFY ME

No soul, no soulmate. Until her...

Jett~

I know full well I don't get to even feel love, much less fall in it.

No soul, no soulmate. Ever.

I don't have room for stolen kisses and fantasies of of making her mine. I've got to break the curse on my brethren and take down the King of Hell.

So why is the dragon part of me insisting on marking and claiming this strange and beautiful woman who just walked into my life (and drank my beer)?

Yvaine~

Really weird stuff is happening, like how I accidentally keep turning this hot guy into a dragon and how I really, really wants to kiss him. Again.

What am I thinking? Dark and broody bad boys with those kind of six-pack abs only want one thing, and they don't want it from me and my big ole butt.

We're stuck together until we can figure out how to break some crazy supernatural curse on me.

But what if I don't want the curse broken?

If you love your shifters broody & hot, your heroines curvy & sassy, and can hardly wait for a feel good Happy Ever After, read this book now!

DRAGONS AND OTHER GOOD LUCK CHARMS

Fucking dragons.

And their fucking mates. Who were all beautiful brave women each of which he had more than a little crush on. If he hadn't seen what finding a soulmate had done for those stupid Wyvern bastards with his own eyes he wouldn't be such a miserable asshole. Now all he could think about was getting a soul shard, finding a mate, and getting the boost in power that came with. It was the only way to save his brothers.

Save himself.

You do one little favor for the most powerful warriors on the planet and they think your soul is redeemable. No matter how much Jett wanted that to be true, it was never going to happen. He poured himself another drink and downed it, liking the burn. It wasn't as hot as his dragon fire, or as satisfying, but for some gods-forsaken reason he came to this little pub night after night waiting on that damned magic dealer to return and in the meantime, tried to get drunk.

No one here tried to manipulate him or wanted anything from him. It was nice and quiet and as mind numbing as ancient Latin. For decades, all his years spent in hell, he'd wished for normalcy. Now that he had it, he was miserable. Maybe he should pick a fight. At least that would be better than crying in his Jägermeister.

He couldn't get into it with a human though. They were too damn fragile. How did these stinking animals even survive in a world where monsters, like demon dragons, were real? Where monsters like he himself were real. No, if he wanted to work off some steam, he needed to find one of those creatures of the night.

His senses told him the group at the nearest table had no powers, although one of them seriously looked like an ogre. Most of the people who lived in this little dot on the map that was Glückstadt, Germany were nothing. That's why it was a good place to hide out. A different kind of presence nipped at the edges of his spidey-senses. Something definitely not human, but with the familiar acrid scent of fire and brimstone. He could find the creature and have some fun hunting it. With his parentage there wasn't anything hellborn he couldn't catch. But it might be more entertaining to see what it was doing here, before he killed it.

The door of the pub blew open and a blonde woman with the glow of something supernatural around her rushed in like the wind had shoved her through the doorway. Jett glanced around to see if anyone else in here noticed how she was lit up like a damned star in the gold night sky.

A few patrons looked her way, but only because of the disturbance. None were taken aback by who or what she was. Not that he had a clue what kind of being hid under her skin. He couldn't be the only one seeing her aura of shiny power. He'd bet a dragon's hoard that whatever beast was here knew and was lying in wait for her.

This should be interesting. Jett picked up his stein and took a long swig, waiting for the scene to play out. If he was lucky, the big bad wolf would make trouble.

The woman pushed her hair out of her face, save one errant strand that she gave a well-practiced blow and then tucked behind her ear. My, oh my. He'd never wanted to be a piece of hair so badly in his life. That mouth was something. She tugged on her t-shirt, that had - shit - a unicorn of all things on it. Any grown woman who wore something like that had an innocence about her that he needed to stay far, far away from.

Her shirt refused to stay in place, and it crept back up, showing the thinnest sliver of skin between it and her jeans. That tiny swathe of her bare side had his cock standing up and taking notice. Which was strange. It wasn't like he had seen, tasted, caressed, and spanked a whole lot more flesh than that.

Jett readjusted his legs, spreading them wide under the table to give his brand new erection some relief from the zipper of his jeans. Then he leaned back in his chair waiting for the action to start. And it would. The masked hell's beast had taken notice of her presence too.

Blondie caught him staring at her and headed straight to his table. Uh-oh. She was going to bring the trouble to him. He'd been laying low for a while, ever since he'd helped Cage, the stupid Gold Wyvern, rescue his mermaid mate from Hell and gotten his own ass kicked by the Black Dragon in the process. Jett would be back for his father's head soon enough. Once he had what he needed to free his brethren.

Blondie made her way through the rest of the patrons and plonked down in the chair next to him. Not across, not on the other side, but so close his arm brushed up against hers as she picked up his half full mug of beer and took two, three, four long gulping swallows.

His cock once again was jealous of an inanimate object. Jett watched her, fascinated. He didn't exactly radiate friendly, come sit with me vibes. The opposite, if his entire life up until now was any proof.

She plonked the now empty stein down on the table and burped. "Pretend to be my boyfriend." She looked back at the door, then at him, her lavender eyes sparkling. "You know, my big bad, very possessive boyfriend."

He'd never in his life seen anyone with eyes like hers. They were mesmerizing. But not enough that he was willing to do something dumb like try to protect her from whatever was chasing her. "And why would I do that?"

"Don't ask. Just kiss me." She glanced back at the door again and the next second it flew open again. Then she slid her fingers into his hair and planted her lips on his.

Jett caught a glimpse of two men with too many muscles not to be supernatural beings shove their way into the room. And he didn't care even a little bit. She touched her mouth to his and the world exploded into fucking rainbows. There could be dragon warriors come to lop off his head, or the Black Dragon himself hunting him down- none of the above would get him to pay any attention to them. Because this was the best fucking kiss he'd ever experienced in his entire miserable life and all she'd done so far was brush her lips across his in a chaste tease.

Not that he spent a lot of time going around kissing people. He'd spent more of his above ground time with the succubae of Geshtianna's coven trying to lure him into their beds than looking for bed partners of his own. Not a single talented succubus had even come close to blowing his mind like this soft, supple, sweet woman licking over his bottom lip asking him to open for her.

Her eyes fluttered shut and the tiniest whimpered moan from her hit him low and hard in the gut. He wrapped an arm around her waist and pulled her in closer wanting to feel the heat of her body touching his. She was warm and soft, her ample curves molded to his hard angles. His fingers found their way to that bit of skin he'd been dying to touch.

She was so damn soft, so fucking sweet.

He didn't do soft. Or sweet. He took what he wanted, when he wanted it.

But not with her. He would give this woman anything she wanted, any time that she wanted it. He'd give her everything if he could. Not that he had much to give.

The sound of a throat being cleared tried its best to break into Jett's living fantasy. "Ahem."

Damn it. This goddess was mere centimeters away from pushing her tongue into his mouth so he could finally taste her, and some asshole was going to interfere. He would simply have to kill them. He very gently broke the kiss but moved his lips only far enough away from hers to speak. "Go away. We're busy."

Jett breathed in her scent. She was snow and sunshine, morning dew on fluffy kittens. Shit. Where did that even come from? Whatever spell she was working on him had turned his brain into mush. Kittens. He didn't even like Grumpy Cat, much less mewling little fur balls.

Blondie had reopened her eyes, but her lips were parted waiting for him to kiss her once again. He brushed that strand of hair off her face and pushed a hand gently into her locks. His body said take, but his mind, and something else he couldn't identify, told him to treat her like a fragile glass ornament.

"Ah, Ah, Ahem."

This person did not understand they were endangering their own life. "What part of go away don't you understand?"

The interrupter, who turned out to be the barmaid named Ninsy who always served him here rolled her eyes and whispered, "You two might want to take that somewhere else. Because those mermen are going to throw a whole lot more than cold water on you."

Jett glanced at the men. Mers. He never did like those guys. Way too full of themselves. Hold up. How did the barmaid know they were not just a couple of strong arms? He'd never detected anything supernatural about her. Maybe she was a witch who used a dampening spell.

He'd be rethinking his choice in watering hole if that were true. He had no love for magical women of any kind. Except whatever the woman in his arms was. He still had no idea. Only that he wanted and needed her. Needed to keep her safe. "Come on, sweet thing. Let's get you out of here."

There was a back entrance he'd used a time or two to avoid other supernaturals. His gasthaus wasn't far. They could continue their kiss and he'd do all the fun and naughty things a pretend boyfriend should do to her there.

"Thanks, but you've provided enough of a distraction. Sorry." She shrugged.

"You don't have to apologize. I thoroughly enjoyed it. " In fact, he'd like to do it a whole lot more.

"Oh, I'm not sorry about that." She pecked him on the cheek and then twisted out of his arms and ducked.

A fat scaly fist slammed into his face in the exact spot her lips had been only a second before. He fell backward, bowling over a whole row of wooden barstools. Very few beings got the drop on him. It was how he'd stayed alive in the depths of Hell as long as he had. He laid on the floor for a second, wondering what the fuck had just happened. He'd honed his fighting skills even more than what his demon of a mother had taught him. Living among succubae and incubae wasn't exactly a walk in the park and those blood suckers had been good training partners. Living with a coven of sex slaves was better than feigning that he was a mindless drone under the Black Witch's spell. For example, if he was bespelled he wouldn't be able to do this.

Jett blew a burst of flames at his attacker's face, lighting the merman's blue hair on fire. The damn fool slapped at his head and ran around the pub unwittingly stoking the flames. Dumbass.

Now, where had blondie gone?

An all-out brawl broke out in the pub and if he didn't find her quickly, she might get hurt. He jumped up on top of a table and surveyed the room for her almost luminescent hair and lush body. Aha. There she was. He expected to find her hiding in a corner, but she was moving through the fracas like a ninja. She bobbed and weaved, spinning around, under, and past the fists being thrown.

Not only could the woman kiss, she could move. Not a single punch even came close to her. While everyone else was diving into the fray, she made her way to the door. Except there were two very large burly men engaged in battle in front of the exit. No way she was getting out that way unless he helped her.

Jett jumped over tables and chairs and even considered pulling out his wings to fly over everyone's heads so he could get to her faster. She was within a meter of the men now and it looked even less likely that they were simply going to let her pass. She paused a half a meter away from them and crossed her arms. Behind her a very loud screaming woman jumped on someone else's back and pulled at his hair steering him like a pony right toward blondie.

They were going to barrel into her, and she was standing there staring at the two men blocking the door. Shit. She was trapped and they were all going to collide. She would be crushed. Jett put on a burst of speed and jumped off someone's shoulders flying through the air toward her and the oncoming disaster.

As he careened over the tops of the brawlers, time slowed. Blondie turned and looked up at him, winked and moved toward the men. She reached her hand forward, pulled something out of the bigger of the two men's pocket and slipped between them and out the door.

Jett crashed into the men, who attacked him for breaking in on their fight. It took him a good fifteen minutes to beat them off and extricate himself from the pub. By then there was no sight of his little kissing ninja thief. He didn't need to be able to see her to find her. He had her soft intricate scent. As did whatever other creatures of the night were stalking her.

He rubbed his hands together. The chase was on and it was going to be fun.

ALSO BY AIDY AWARD

Dragons Love Curves

Chase Me

Tease Me

Bite Me

Cage Me

Baby Me

More Dragons coming soon!

Fated for Curves

A Curvy Girl Sci-fi Romance Series

A Touch of Fate

A Tangled Fate

A Twist of Fate

A Taste of Fate (coming soon)

The Curvy Love Series

Curvy Diversion

Curvy Temptation

Curvy Persuasion

Curvy Domination (coming soon)

The Curvy Seduction Saga

Rebound

Rebellion

Reignite

ABOUT THE AUTHOR

Aidy Award is a curvy girl who kind of has a thing for stormtroopers. She's also the author of the popular Curvy Love series and the hot new Dragons Love Curves series. She writes curvy girl erotic romance, about real love, and dirty fun, with happy ever afters because every woman deserves great sex and even better romance, no matter her size, shape, or what the scale says.

Read the delicious tales of hot heroes and curvy heroines come to life under the covers and between the pages of Aidy's books. Then let her know because she really does want to hear from her readers.

Connect with Aidy on her website. www.AidyAward.com and join her
Facebook Group - Aidy's Amazeballs.

Made in the USA
Middletown, DE
03 June 2023